Alphas' Origins

An Iron Beast Pack Novella

Angelica Aquiles

ALPHAS' ORIGINS

Copy/Line Editing: Heather Fox at Fox Proof Editing

Cover Design: Francesca Michelon at MerryBookRound

Formatting by: The Nutty Formatter

To my husband and kids for giving me the time to create worlds.

Preface

Please know this is a Novella not a full length novel. Kat will not appear in this book. This is guys' origins and what led them to become Alphas.

There is reference to abuse that may cause triggers. Please proceed with caution.

This book contains adult content and mature language. It is intended for readers 18+.

Enjoy!

The night our pack was pillaged by hunters, the Alphas and Betas abandoned us. I saw them running for the hills behind our house, but it was too late to tell the others. There was so much blood, screaming, and chaos. One of my mothers held my little sister as she cried beneath the kitchen table, and I watched from the window in the bedroom as men on horses set fire to our farms.

My father was out there trying to find my other mother, but I'd lost sight of him as he shifted into his wolf and disappeared into the fight.

After hours of carnage, the sun cast its golden rays across the smoldering remains of our land, and the Alphas and Betas were back to assess the damage and count the bodies.

Our pack needed answers, retribution, someone to place blame on, and the Alphas lifted a finger at the only house left standing. Ours. It was luck that saved us, but our Alphas insisted we were working with the hunters.

My father fought gallantly beside his pack while our leaders fled to safety, but it was too easy for our community to believe the Alphas' lies when we lost so little compared to the other families.

They cast the five of us into the cold, and our broken community joined surrounding packs to rebuild their lives without us.

Though some shifters do, we would never consider working with hunters to hurt our people, but it was easier to point a finger at us than to admit their leaders failed to keep them safe. Our word means nothing against theirs, and no pack would take us in once their lies got around.

We are a family of vagrants now, and our parents hunt the woods relentlessly to provide what they can. But the winter this year is harsh, and there isn't much game as the temperature drops. If I were just a year older, I would be sixteen and able to shift and help my parents hunt, but instead, I'm usually left to guard my little sister when they have to leave us.

Our fire crackles and burns low as we settle down for the evening with nothing to eat, and a deep sadness creases my little sister's face as the sounds of the nearby circus carry over the field.

Our new life has been the hardest for Zoe, drifting from place to place and hiding what we are. She's only ten years old, and the child-like light in her eyes dims more each day.

My mothers and father are tough, never showing her how worried they are to be out here on our own without protection, but I see it in the glances they exchange over our meager meals.

We weren't wealthy members of the pack before, but we had enough. Now our bellies growl, and our teeth chatter against the wind as we listen to children laughing and music playing, taunting us with a normal life just out of reach.

I can't see myself staying in one place or trusting another

pack to be my home, but my sister craves the familiarity of pack life, and I can see how helpless my parents must feel.

A faint melody drags across the field to where we sit quietly around the fire, and I hum a song I heard a long time ago. As the words come back to me, I sing louder, watching the lines on little Zoe's face ease into a smile. I'm not sure if I'm remembering the lyrics correctly, but the words feel right.

My sister's eyes close as she leans into me, and I hope she can pretend for a moment she's sitting beneath the canvas tent with the wealthy families, warm with a belly full of sweets as the music plays. I sing to her until tears gather along her lashes, and she buries her face in my lap and falls asleep.

We rise with the sun and pack up, knowing it's too risky to stay in one place for too long. My sister begs to hear one more song as we prepare for travel, and as I oblige her every wish, a man's voice startles me. "You have a beautiful voice."

A tall, burly man approaches from the woods, and my nose immediately catches his scent. He's another shifter, not a wolf like us, but a lion.

My mother, Olivia, grabs my shoulder. "What do you want?" She places her body in front of me like a shield, and I can hear the tremble in her voice.

Shifters have been disappearing for months, and without a pack to keep us safe, my mothers have been anxious when strangers cross our paths.

"I was just complimenting your son's voice." Soft footsteps approach behind me, and I turn to find my other mother, Emily, at my back with Zoe clutching her hand. My father reaches for Olivia, and we stand together, staring at the strange man.

Sensing our wariness, he continues, "I see you guys are packing up. If you don't have a place to go—"

"We have a place," my father snaps.

The stranger looks at our belongings packed up, and it's obvious he recognizes us for what we are. Drifters. No sane family of shifters would be out here alone in the winter if they had somewhere concrete to call home.

"I would still like to extend our circus to you all. Your son has a melodious voice. He can bring in hundreds and thousands of people." He stares off, and I think he's imagining all the money he believes I can make him. He looks at my parents again. "We're a family here, and we'll treat you as such. We all have a part to play in the circus, and we get along fairly well."

My parents look at each other, and I see the doubt on their faces.

"All of you will have a place to stay with us. We protect one another. We're a family, and we can be yours too." His smile widens like he knows that's exactly what we're looking for—a place to belong.

My parents are sharing a wordless conversation, and though I've never been able to understand them, I can see the longing in my mothers' eyes. I guess it's kind of like when my sister and I talk to each other without actually speaking. We just know what the other is thinking.

Olivia breaks the silence. "We would like to meet the people you call family and decide once we've gotten a chance to know them."

"Of course. I would expect nothing less. My name is Henry, by the way."

"My name is Olivia. That's my wife, Emily, and my husband, Carter." She points to me. "The one with the beautiful voice is my son Benjamin, and this is our daughter, Zoe."

"It's very nice to meet you all." Henry nods once before turning around and motioning for us to follow.

We meet every single person and learn the parts they play, and though I know what Henry expects from me, I wonder what tasks my sister and parents will be given to contribute.

We are all outcasts from different magical origins. Shifters, Faeries, Witches, and Demons, all living as one family.

A place for all of us to belong.

My sister's eyes light up at the possibility of having a new pack and a family, so I know whatever I have to do here will be worth her happiness alone.

The day speeds along as we meet everyone and learn the ropes, and by the time the sun sinks below the tree line, our parents have made their decision to stay.

We're finally home again.

The whip comes down on my back again, and I clench my jaw waiting for another lash to sear my flesh. I've lost count of how many times he has raised his hand to me. Twelve? Twenty? All I know for sure is my back burns, and fresh blood trickles down my sides.

The kitchen table feels cool against my chest, and I try to focus on that sensation and hold still. If I move or whine in the slightest, my father will continue to punish me for not being wolf enough to take it.

It's the same story every time he gets this drunk, so I wrap my arms around two of the table's corners and stay here until my body can no longer hold me in this position. My legs tremble beneath me as his hand comes down in another devastating blow. I try to catch my slipping body, but my palms are slick with sweat against the wood.

When I turn eighteen and am finally free of my father, I will no longer be weak. My wolf is with me now, peeking out from below the surface, biding his time until we can leave this shack and never look back.

"You worthless mutt," my father yells. "It should have

been you, not my Isla." His voice cracks as sharply as the whip across my skin, reminding me I'm the reason his mate died.

My birth was the catalyst in losing everything he loved. He was the only mate of my mother's that didn't die of grief after I was cut from her womb. He lost the love of his life and his brothers because I was born. He drowns his loneliness in Faerie wine because he can't stand the sight of me breathing the air I don't deserve.

When I was little, he found me crying over a letter my mother wrote to me before I was born, and he ripped it from my hands and tore it to pieces. He said I had no right to mourn the loss of the woman I took from him. That was the first time I felt the sting of his whip.

I crank my neck and look around the little shack my father and I were banished to. The pack leaders live in lavish homes and never go without, but the rest of us have nothing but scraps to live off of, doomed to be slaves for the Alphas and Betas.

If you weren't born in the lap of luxury, you have to earn your keep with labor and skill, but it shouldn't be this way. Our loyalty to our pack should be enough to earn the right to decent living conditions. The Alphas should be taking care of us instead of making us beg for food and essentials. Even our shifting and hunting are restricted here, the very fiber of who we are.

My father was a revered hunter before I was born, but when his drinking became a problem after my mother died, we fell to the bottom rung of our pack in an instant. It doesn't stop them from calling on him to use his skills to track the hunters after us; they just no longer compensate him with the same money or respect.

We're nothing special here, and the kids of the Alphas

and Betas make sure I don't forget my place. I made the mistake once of saying *When I become an Alpha of the pack.* They laughed and mocked me until they were red in the face, but even if they aren't aware of my mounting strength, I can feel it.

One of the Betas started noticing what the others failed to see, and sometimes I catch him following me. He thinks he's discreet, but I hear his footsteps and sense his presence. I may not be able to take them down yet, but I plan to one day, including my father.

"You ruined my life," he slurs, the Faerie wine buzzing through his system, one thousand times more potent than the regular alcohol humans drink.

He gives me five more lashes before he slumps over a chair to catch his breath. My blood seeps to the floor, and I watch with wobbly legs as red liquid pools around my bare and swollen feet.

One day I'll escape, and one day I'll become the Alpha.

Just two more years I chant to myself before my father straightens and lands the whip between my raw shoulders. My vision blurs until everything fades to black.

"Oh, Ash." The soft and tender voice of my friend wakes me. My lashes feel heavy, and it takes a couple of tries before I can open my eyes. The ache on my back makes it hard for me to look up. I only see her tattered wool skirt hanging around her dirty, bare feet until she kneels on the floor.

My father didn't attempt to move me to the bed. But again, he never does. He always leaves me in a pool of blood and vomit. Like the carcass of a wounded animal, discarded and left for the vultures.

I lick my dry, cracked lips before opening my mouth, but when I try to speak, nothing comes out. After a few more tries, my words finally claw their way up my raw throat. "I can't move."

"You want me to kill him?" Her seriousness makes me laugh. I've grown up with Krissy and her sister Amara on the outskirts of the pack lands, and though Krissy is an incredible witch, she's not a murderer.

"Nah, he'll eventually get what he deserves." Maybe even by my hand if I find the nerve to stand up for myself. I try again to get up on my own, but my arms shake, and I slump back against the table again.

She cringes, which makes me worry more. When I try to move again, she gently puts her warm hand on my arm to stop me. "I'm going to heal you," she says. Changing into my wolf form would help my body heal faster, but I'm forbidden to shift without approval from our Alphas. Krissy knows I can't help myself when I'm this busted up, but she's always here to lend her powers. "It's going to feel hot and sting a little, but it will help you get up and moving."

I don't get to say anything before a familiar pressure builds on my back. She always cures me when my father does his worst, but only enough to get me back on my feet. She knows if she restores my wounds completely, it will earn me double the lashes next time.

"Thanks, Krissy. I owe you one."

Her cheeks burn as she lowers her gray eyes with a small smile. "Don't mention it, Ash. I hate that he does this to you."

I grab her hands and give them a light squeeze. "I'm going to leave one day, Krissy, and when I come back, I'm going to take over the pack. You mark my words." She nods in encouragement because she knows what it will mean to her family when I rise to power.

They've lived as outcasts here like I have, surviving on whatever the Alphas and Betas think they are worth. We both know too well what it means to be walked on and dismissed, and I want to be the one to offer her family a better life here. I know my dear friend will always be by my side.

CHAPTER 3

Az (1816)

My stomach rumbles loudly, reminding me it's been four days since I've had my last ration.

Clients take their pick of us from where we stand, lined against a wall and staring blankly ahead. They come in dressed expensive, wearing clean leather boots and hard expressions. They speak quietly to Madam, never making eye contact until a bedroom door slams behind them. The clients pay double for discretion, but we never see a single coin for what we endure.

Mr. Hank—the man in charge of keeping us in line—withholds food and clothing to motivate and punish us. He says we have a debt to pay, and when we're all paid up, we are free to go, but freedom never seems to come. I used to wish for the day the clients were bored of me and no longer called my number, but now I wonder if it's freedom or death that awaits me on the other side of the front door.

Most of us were picked up off the streets when we were kids. We were accustomed to cleaning shops, working as farm hands, or in dark factories when Mr. Hank found us. He promised a much better wage to work for him, and because the job was so far, he offered us food and a place to sleep with decent wages sent home to our families.

I don't remember much about my parents. They disappeared when I was very young, but I was lucky enough to find a group of friends to take me in. We were squatters living on an unclaimed piece of land on the outskirts of town. Many of us crammed into a one-room hovel that didn't do much to keep out the cold or rain, and every day I'd walk miles into town for work.

I was so excited to start my new job that I didn't even go back to say goodbye. Sometimes when I'm at my lowest, a memory hits me of an older girl I lived with who tried to take care of us like a mother would, singing songs to distract the younger ones from the pangs of hunger that kept us awake at night. But then the memory is gone, and I'm alone again, wondering if I'm making up these images to feel loved and missed by someone.

I was gullible and young when I came here, but it didn't take long to figure out we were prisoners. We would never see the money we thought we'd be earning. I'd give anything to work a factory job again, bringing home a little bit of money at the end of the week with pride.

There is no pride in what they force us to do here.

Today is my sixteenth birthday, at least I think it is. My body feels weak and sickly from not eating, but there's something else there as well, something different that makes my skin ripple with anticipation. I've been hot and dizzy all week like maybe I'm coming down with something, and today it's worse than ever.

My bedroom is tiny, with just enough space for a large, dirty mattress pushed against the wall and an empty fireplace that has never seen warmth. Four other boys sleep here, all in one bed with a single blanket.

I try to take a turn resting on the mattress while I'm alone, but my stomach growls and twists in hunger, and I have to find something to eat today. I crawl out from under the blanket and creep down the hall, trying my best to go unnoticed. I'm not well-liked here, and if the others see me, I don't know if I'm strong enough to withstand their abuse today. Jesse and John are the worst, and I look for their taunting faces around every corner.

As I walk down the stairs, my senses are assaulted by an expensive perfume, marjoram flowers, and rosemary, and I know Madam has been here recently. I've always been able to pick up on oils and fragrances, and I wonder why the others aren't as perceptive.

I sag into a chair at an empty table in the kitchen, and as if they have been waiting for me, John and Jesse fall into the surrounding seats with smug smiles. My body tenses immediately, and I fist my hands into the hem of the only shirt I have left.

John and Jesse are too big to fit the clothes they take from me, but possessions are the only form of money most of us have, and the more things you have to barter with, the better off you'll fare in the long run.

Madam insists we are family here, and she calls these Neanderthals my brothers, but family shouldn't take joy in seeing you suffer the way they do, even if their hatred grew from jealousy.

It all started when they noticed the extra piece of bread I get every month, but what they don't know is what that extra piece of food has cost me in blood.

A man comes in every four weeks—a man with weird tastes and the money to back them. He likes to tie me up and physically hurt me. My body bruises for a week or more.

Some of my wounds don't even heal before he's back to do it all over again.

The man gets angry because my cock never gets hard, but if I'm being honest, it never has.

After the last beating I took, I told Mr. Hank I never wanted to take that client again. He laughed in my face, assuring me if someone with money has their eye on me—regardless of their twisted tastes—I will do whatever the fuck they ask.

Since our first encounter, I've never been the same, and my stomach revolts when another person touches me. I avoid the crowds of my *brothers*. I've resorted to sleeping in a corner just because I don't want to share a bed with the others. I hyperventilate when it's my turn to work.

Thankfully, no other *weird* requests have come in, at least not for me. I don't chat with anyone else about my clients or theirs. Talking about the abuse and humiliation only makes it harder to forget.

John and Jesse aren't like me. They came here on their own with nowhere else to go as children. I've heard a million different stories as to why they are paid wages and allowed to come and go, most of them about the things they do for Mr. Hank in private.

They have been Madam's lapdogs for as long as I've been here, always watching us and reporting back when we steal food or try to escape, and since the day I arrived, they've made it their mission to terrorize me every chance they get. I've been kicked, beaten, and bullied, and even though I've tried to keep out of their way, I'm their favorite target.

"Aziel, fancy seeing you here so early for dinner." Jesse chuckles while twirling the expensive knife a client gave him as a gift. John's lips curl into an evil grin in anticipation. My body shivers in response to their proximity.

They know I haven't eaten in days, yet they're still here terrorizing me. Today is different, though. I don't have the patience for the abuse. I'm exhausted and hungry, and my body and mind aren't up to it.

"Don't you have a client to entertain?" I face Jesse, but I'm talking to both of them. I finished my last client hours ago. I told Mr. Hank today was my birthday, and surprisingly, he told me to take a break. I suspect it has more to do with how weak and sick I look and nothing to do with him showing kindness. Most clients won't look twice at someone so sickly and droopy. No one has acknowledged my birthday, and I'm sure I'll have to make up for my time off tomorrow.

"We wanted to hang out with you on your *birthday*." The way Jesse says *birthday* sounds more like he's mocking me. I try to get up and leave, but he pushes me back down. The way he grabs my shoulder makes me squirm, but I try to remain still.

Calm, deep breaths, I tell myself. If I freak out, that'll just give them more ammunition against me.

I need to eat. I feel hot, and my patience is running thin. I look down at my hands as intense pain shoots through each finger and up to my elbows. The pain intensifies as I shake and clench them, frantically looking for relief. I watch in horror as my skin splits and bone-like talons poke through the tips of my fingers.

What the fuck? Am I hallucinating now?

I hide my hands underneath the table and look up to see if they've noticed. They're still talking shit and laughing, which means I'm probably just going crazy. How many days can you go without food before insanity hits?

My vision starts to blur, and now I know something is seriously wrong with me. I try to stand up, but my balance fails, and when I slam back into the chair, the legs splinter and break with a loud boom, sending me to the floor in a pile of debris.

"You're going to have to pay for that." John sounds like a hyena as he laughs, and I have to cover my ears as I fly to my feet and make a break toward the hallway.

"Hey, where are you going?" Jesse shouts. "We aren't done with you."

I make my way out of the kitchen and up the stairs, leaving the howls of laughter behind. Feeling safe inside my room, I slam the door and lean my back against it, sliding to the floor. Everything spins uncontrollably, and as I try to cover my eyes, the long claws protruding from my fingers grab my attention.

What's happening to me?

My heart thumps loudly, and I can hear it in my ears. I fall on my hands and knees, dry heaving, but since I haven't eaten in days, nothing comes out.

My body thrashes against my will, and a sharp, twisting pain sparks fire in every cell in my body. I can hardly breathe as the room seems to shrink around me, and I briefly think how unfair it is to die on my birthday.

When I open my tear-filled eyes, the only clothes I have left are torn to shreds on the floor in front of me, and my vision is so sharp I can see the tiny threads woven through each piece of fabric.

My hands are huge paws against the stained floor, and when I try to stand, I tower over the mattress next to me.

There are no mirrors in my room, but I can feel the animalistic urge to lean my head back and howl, and the small voice I sometimes hear in my head feels louder than ever.

I don't know what I am or what's happening to me, but it feels like I'm finally becoming what I was meant to be.

"About time," the voice in my head howls in excitement.

Is this some kind of dream or have I finally lost it?

"I'm your wolf. I'm a part of you. I've been hiding in the shadows, patiently waiting to come out." It replies back to me.

I make my way to the window on four legs instead of two, and I wonder if the jump from the roof would kill me if I tried to escape. I can't just walk through the house like this. I'd probably be killed on sight.

The adrenaline coursing through my veins drowns out my fear of heights as I push against the window and watch it swing open. It's already getting dark outside, and I take in a lung full of fresh air before leaping.

All four of my feet hit the ground gracefully, and I look out over the dim street before me. Freedom. It's all I've ever wanted, and my stomach roars painfully with the need to eat.

Everything smells stronger, the rotting trash behind the house, the stench of rats creeping through the dark street corners, the men occupying bedrooms just on the other side of these shabby walls. Resisting the urge to break down the front door, I take off, sticking to the shadows as I hunt for my next meal.

After eating more than I ever have in my lifetime, I find myself stark naked, staring at the same rundown brick prison I thought I'd never see again. I don't know why I came back here or what I'm waiting on until the front door creaks open, and a smug man with a walking cane pauses in shock.

"This is why," a voice in my head laughs. *"We're taking back our life."* I thought the voice in my head would fade once my body went back to normal, but I was wrong.

The man's not smiling anymore as he takes in my lack of clothing, but the long claws still protruding from my hands cause him to raise his cane and edge around me warily. He's used to seeing young boys on display for his sick enjoyment, and I picture slicing through his throat with my claws and ending his miserable life, but a familiar scent wafting through the open door makes me forget about the man limping away in a hurry.

I'm still trying to rationalize what's happening to me, but my limbs feel so much stronger after eating, and they propel me forward, back into the house of horrors.

The parlor is empty when I walk in, and I follow the smell of sex and fear into the hall of bedrooms. The first order of business is finding some clothes. Jesse and John share a room with a few others, and going through their belongings sends a thrill through me. I find the finest pair of trousers and look for a clean top. After pulling on the oversized clothes, I grab a pair of shoes on my way out.

Heavy footsteps in the hall send a new spark of adrenaline shooting through me as I pause and listen carefully—the corners of my mouth quirking up.

"Let's finish him off," my wolf says, ready for a fight. He's been watching in the shadows, waiting patiently to come out. I just didn't know what it was at the time, until now.

"What are you doing here?" Jesse hisses. I turn around slowly, my vision sharpening and focusing on the way his lower lip quivers as he feigns bravery. He can't take his eyes off my claws, and I can't seem to control them.

I tilt my head to the side, looking for his weaknesses, but now that he's the little man, I see many. I should have looked for them before, but I was too afraid to stand up for myself.

"What the hell is wrong with you?" He backs away slowly, eyes wide and fearful. "Did you make a deal with the devil?" I stay silent, slowly stalking my prey. "I'm . . . I'm not afraid of you," he whispers. I lift my nose, breathing in the scent of fear and piss, with satisfaction.

His eyes widen and my blood pulses. I'm the predator and he's my prey. *"Why have we waited so long to do this?"* The voice in my head becomes an image I can see perfectly, *a* wolf poised in the darkest corner of my mind, ready to take down the coward in front of us. I can feel my wolf's excitement inside me like a separate being, but having Jesse under my grip excites me too.

"What would happen if we messed up that pretty face of his?" my wolf asks, and I'm just as intrigued as he is. He's pretty; I'll give him that. It's the reason his clients are always willing to buy him anything he desires.

"I don't know, but I'm curious to find out," I reply.

"W-who . . ." he stutters. "Who are you talking to?" I guess I accidentally said that one out loud. I back him up against the wall just outside of his room. His palms are flat as he tries to hold on to something.

His eyes widen when my clawed hand brushes across his cheek. He squirms and pleads, "No. Please, no. You can't do this to me." He's nice to look at. That's the only reason anyone likes this piece of shit.

I run my talons across his silky, pale skin until he tries to push back, but he's trapped. "I won't tell anyone you're a freak."

"Freak?" my wolf bites out.

"You're here by choice, helping to keep dozens of children locked up and abused daily, and you think I'm the freak?"

"Okay, fuck. I know! We'll help them get out if they want, okay? I'll give out extra rations if they want to stay. I'll do anything, Aziel, please." Aziel. I fucking hate that name.

Every time it's uttered, I see the man I've grown to hate hovering over me with his whip, getting off on bruising and splitting my flesh.

"From now on, my name is Az." The name I was born with is dirty and tainted, and that part of me is dead now.

"Yeah, fine. Whatever. I'll call you whatever you want, but please let me go," he cries, but I don't feel sorry for him. He and his friends made Aziel's life a living hell for years, but Az is done taking their shit.

I run one claw across his face, and he hisses in pain. When the smell of copper hits my nose, my adrenaline pumps with excitement. I stare at the blood pooling from his cheek, and without even thinking, I stick my tongue out and lick the wound.

"You think you're tough now, you sick bastard?" he shouts, trying but failing to sound gallant. He thinks I'm the monster, but I've never terrorized anyone. I've only kept to myself. "My friends and I should have killed you when we had the chance."

With one swipe, blood pools from his neck, and he no longer tries to contain his fear. He screams for help, but we've all learned to ignore those cries of pain and desperation echoing down the halls. No one helps anyone but themselves here.

The smell of sweet terror permeates the room when he realizes no one is coming for him.

Being a predator comes naturally to me, and I want more.

I rip his top off and run my talons across his soft flesh. He writhes against me, squeezing his eyes shut. After all the shit he's put me through, I don't feel bad, and there's no way I'm turning back now. If I let him live, no one will ever want him again.

When he least expects it, I slash my claws across his

upper body. There's a sharp inhale before more blood gushes from the gaping wounds. I rub my hand through the liquid and bring it to his face. He avoids looking at my hand, focusing on my chin and his hard breathing instead.

I bring my palm close to my mouth and hold his forehead still, forcing him to watch me lick through each of my digits. I can only imagine what I look like, grinning maniacally with blood staining my lips and chin. I probably look like a deranged psycho, but I don't mind it one bit.

"We need to get out of here before someone hears us." My wolf is right—as much as I want to keep playing, we need to leave now.

I tilt my head to the side, watching him shake uncontrollably. "Look at me." My voice sounds foreign, more confident. His chin wobbles as he tilts his head down instead. "I said look at me," I shout. He drags his eyes up, and I see the fear and regret as he realizes I've decided his fate.

With the flick of my wrist, I rip his heart out and drop his body to the floor. So much for letting him live.

A pool of blood surrounds his limp body, and I casually turn from him and continue gathering the rest of his clothes. It's not like he'll be using them anyway, and his wardrobe was always in better condition than mine.

I make my way downstairs, walking past the empty parlor and into the kitchen where no one would see me leave. I've stared at this back door for years, dying to take off when Mr. Hank was taking his pick from the lineup of workers. But the only kid I knew who got out was hunted down and brought back in binds, and when Mr. Hank finished punishing him in front of us, he died on the parlor floor.

"Where do you think you're going?" John asks, blocking my exit. His smirk tells me all I need to know. He thinks they'll be beating me up again. No more. I'm a wolf, even if I have no clue how. "Oh, your ass is going to be in trouble," he taunts. "Those are Jesse's clothes. He's going to beat the shit out of you if he knows you took them." He folds his arms and leans against the door, watching me with so much hate.

"I doubt that," I say as I walk past him, but he brings his arm up to hold me hostage.

"Move." It's low, but he can't miss the threat.

"Oh, it looks like Aziel has grown some balls," he chuckles loudly.

"Kill him," my wolf pushes. My vision grows sharper, and I know my eyes have changed when I hear him gasp and take a small step back.

"He put us through so much shit. He deserves to die."

I narrow my eyes, and he takes another step back.

"It's Az now," I tell him as I snatch Jesse's knife from his fingers and plunge it straight into his eyeball. He screams louder than Jesse did, and I know I have to get the fuck out of here now.

"Fuck you, Aziel. I will fucking kill you!" he screams as he covers his bloody eye with the palm of his hand. Now it's my turn to chuckle and make my way out, not bothering to put him out of his misery.

"What's going—" Before he can finish, I use the knife to stab the newcomer in the throat. A crowd begins to form in the kitchen, but no one dares to get close to me.

"Kill him," John says, still crying about his fucking eye. I look around, but no one moves an inch. They look at my bag and then my claws.

I walk out of the kitchen to make my way to the front door. Everyone gives me a wide berth, unwilling to be the next body in my way.

I twist the knob, but before I can leave, a voice calls, "Where do you think you're going, Aziel." I put my bag down and face Madam. Her long black hair sits in a knot at the top of her head, and her extravagant hoop skirt gives her wide hips an even wider appearance. She has a soft voice but a mean backhand, and though some of the boys call her momma, she's the very definition of evil. "You have an important client coming to see you later tonight." I turn to face her, but she doesn't even blink when she looks at my eyes or claws, and I question her calm demeanor when staring into the face of a monster. Does she know what I am? Is she like me?

I laugh darkly, no longer feeling afraid to talk back. "If he's such an important client of yours, you blow him."

"What is going on with you?" she spits, clearly annoyed and not at all concerned for my health or safety. "I need you to get your room ready." She glosses over what I said and pretends she still holds power here.

"No."

"No? You little shit, you listen to me." She grabs her whip from her chair and strides toward me, big and brawny for a woman, but weak compared to the wolf baring his teeth inside me. Before she can bring the whip across my face, I grab her hand.

"We will no longer be weak. We are Alphas." My wolf's words are strange, but I can't help agreeing with him.

I grab her arm and twist it until I hear it crack and she howls in pain.

"Make her bleed." My wolf doesn't need to tell me twice. I grab the knife from my pocket, still covered in John's blood, and sink it into her fleshy neck. For the first time, I can feel my cock swelling as I watch her bleed out.

Hmmm . . . I guess blood is the only thing that can make me hard.

Chapter 4

Tyler (1818)

The pressure of always needing to be perfect has exhausted me. The Alphas don't require their children to go through the extensive training I've been through. Not even the other Betas had to go through the preparations I had to deal with.

My parents are wired differently. They're more competitive, fiercer, and they hate being wrong. The only reason they're not Alphas is because the current Alphas know how to keep my family happy. If not, my parents would have demolished them ages ago. My parents are the Betas of The Nightshade Growlers and are well respected in our community.

It's ingrained in me to prove to everyone I'm the best. If I can't win a match, I feel like a total failure, and that's why I never lose . . . . Well, unless it is my dads I have to face. It's hard as shit to beat them.

All four of my dads, my mom, and my brother stand with me at the entrance of a tall brick building. But, it's not just *any* building.

Mystic Shadow Academy sprawls along the upper part of

the building. This place is huge, and it only houses the supernatural. Only the wealthiest families have their kids attend this elite college, and of course, my parents are Betas, which means I have no choice.

No mortal is allowed to get close to this place. They have wards to keep them out. I'll be living here for the next four years, but I'm not here to have a good time like the others at this school. No, it wasn't in the cards for me to ever have fun.

"Tyler, this is it! Everything we've taught you about becoming the Beta of the pack was for this moment," Mateo, one of my four fathers, reminds me. He's a cook in the kitchen and a badass negotiator. "If something happens to us—"

"Dad, don't," I cut him off. I don't like to think of something tragic happening to them, but my parents like to remind me of my duties if anything goes wrong.

Off in the distance, I notice Brandon, Owen, and Dylan bidding their families farewell, and though I've never fit in with their group, they are supposed to be my Beta brothers. Mom thinks attending school here will give us the chance to bond and meet our destined mate, but I have my doubts.

"I can't wait to go here." My only brother, Nick, sighs from beside me as he looks at the building with longing. I try not to flinch or let his words get to me. He's two years younger, and when he attends, he won't have to worry about training for a position he doesn't want. He only has to worry about his classes and having fun before he goes on to become whatever he wants to be in our pack. He has a choice because he is second born.

My parents gave him the same training, but it was never as intensive as mine. Everything was lighter for him because he doesn't have to worry about taking over any legacy. All the pressure is on me to be the best Beta I can be and to serve our Alphas and the pack.

Being a Beta doesn't bug me, but I know I'm meant for something bigger. I love my pack, don't get me wrong. It's one of the better packs around, but I want my own. My heart and wolf both agree that we are meant for something greater than The Nightshade Growlers. But it's not something I'll openly say in front of my parents.

"Tyler, are you feeling alright?" James' soothing voice helps ease some of the tension in my jaw. He's the most level-headed out of my dads. He keeps us all grounded with my mom's help, of course. I look up to all my dads, but he's the most down-to-earth person I know. He breaks up fights and is a scary dude. If he were a stranger, I'd be skeptical to approach him.

"Yeah, we're feeling great. Four years of bonding with those pricks on the horizon, couldn't be better." I try not to giggle at my wolf's words.

"Yeah, yeah. I'm good." I try to slip into my easy-going smile, but James doesn't buy it.

"What are you talking about, James? Of course he's alright. Knowing our Tyler, he's going to be top of his class," Damian says proudly. They're all competitive in their own way, but he's the fiercest out of all of them. He's not combative with us, but the outside world better watch out. You don't want to cross his path.

I've realized I'm the same way, obsessed with being at the top of everything. Though I used to think my competitive streak came from training, it feels more natural than learned, like it's just a part of who I am. That's why being a Beta doesn't sit well with me. My parents may seem happy in their positions in the pack, but I would never be content in their place.

"You remember our training," Rob says. He's the one who taught me hand-to-hand combat. He's the best I've ever seen, and until our sparring match last week, no one had ever taken him down. That moment isn't one I'll soon forget.

The unrelenting rain soaks into my clothes as I stand quietly in the middle of the training arena. With every step, the mud grows deeper and harder to navigate.

Rob circles me like a hunter stalking his prey, his wide smile gleaming with excitement. "Today is the last day to show me you're ready."

"But—" His mouth turns into a hard line, and he shakes his head. I know what he's thinking. No excuses, son. *He tells me that every day after he destroys me in training.*

Excuses are for the weak.

But after everything I've put into training and everything I've given up in my eighteen years, the thought of him telling me I'm not ready for the academy sends rage coursing through me like fire. My entire life has been about training for the academy.

"You know all my moves from a mile away, Dad. I'm ready." Music and laughter drift through the downpour, and I envy the kids whose parents are with them at tonight's celebration. I wish I knew what it felt like to have a father's love and compassion unconditional of my rank in training.

"Show me what you got." He tips his chin to beckon me forward, and I let out a long sigh.

He blocks every blow, catches each fist I hurl at his face and body, and when I sweep a leg through the mud, he grabs my ankle and twists, sending me face-first into the ground.

"Maybe we should keep you home for another year. I don't think you're getting it."

I see red when I fly back to my feet, soaking wet and caked with clay-like dirt.

We fight like never before, both of us panting and bloody before the round is over. It's hard to stand on my swollen leg, but Rob is hurt too. For the first time in my life, he's holding his arm to his chest as if I've broken it, but he doesn't relent.

"You're still playing games, son. You need to start fighting like your life depends on it." His eyes are amber like mine, warring with the need to shift and heal quickly, but that would make him look weak.

I limp forward and lunge at him again, but he sidesteps and laughs as I stumble. "I've fucking had it. If you open yourself up to me again, I'm gonna take it." Claws rip from his hands as he hunkers down and watches me calculate my next move.

I have to do something he doesn't suspect. Using my bad leg, I swing it around and swipe at him from underneath. He falls to the ground hard, and my body sags, the adrenaline finally fading.

Never once in all my years of training with Rob has he ever landed on his back. I drag my feet toward my father, waiting for him to gripe about my form, but he's laughing. His loud, whooping laughter brings a nervous smile to my face as I collapse into the mud next to him.

"You did it, Tyler. You're ready," he says proudly. Tears of relief sting my eyes, and I fall back onto the wet earth, watching the rain tumble down in a sheet of gray.

Rob sits up and rolls his neck, trying to adjust his shoulder and arm. "Resilience is everything, Tyler. When you give up, you're done for."

Mom blocks my view of the school when she turns to face me. I'm really going to miss her. Her light brown eyes shine with unshed tears as she tries to put on a brave face, but as soon as we leave, she's going to break down and cry.

"I'm going to miss you, Tyler." She grabs my cheeks

tenderly, pulling my face lower and kissing me on one of my dimples. Her lavender perfume assaults my nose, but it's warm and comforting at the same time. I snuck a small bottle of her signature scent into the bottom of the bag slung over my shoulder.

"I don't want to be here," I whisper as she pulls away. "I hate these guys." She knows how hard it's been for me to accept the fate of being bound to Brandon, Owen, and Dylan.

Mom chuckles. "They'll grow on you. If—" She looks at each of her husbands and steps closer, murmuring in my ear, "If you don't end up liking them, we'll find you a way out." She winks before pulling away.

I'm left here stunned by my mom's words. She's loyal to The Nightshade Growlers, so I'm taken aback when she tells me she'll find me a way out.

"Darlene," Rob says gently. He grabs my mom by her waist. "He's going to be fine. He's got the most amazing mother who helped guide him and the most badass fathers who have trained him." His words are encouraging, but I'm not so sure about them as I stand before my new home. I hope he's right.

CHAPTER 5

ASH (1818)

I waited for him to stumble home, drink in hand, knowing what kind of mood he'd be in today. My birthday. The day my mother died eighteen years ago as she tried to bring me into this world.

His bloodshot eyes found me instantly when he threw the front door open and swayed inside. He swore and threw his bottle in my direction, but I sat stock still as it cracked against the fireplace behind me, the remnants of his liquor causing the fire to surge higher.

Now we stare at each other, waiting for the other to act first. He wants me to flinch, hunker down, and cower under his large frame. But he doesn't stand so tall these days, and though he senses the shift in power between us, he's hanging on to all his hatred like it's the only thing keeping him alive.

He sees his whip in my hand and stills, weighing his options. "Whatcha gonna do with that, coward? You think you're big and strong now?" Without a word, I rise slowly to my full height and toss his precious whip right into the fireplace. Years of blood soaking into the leather straps, finally gone, withering under the flames.

"You're gonna pay for that in blood, you little shit." He stumbles toward the mantle and finds the hunting knife he keeps there, brandishing it at me. He's desperate to keep me in the chains I've worn my entire life, but his fear is repugnant.

My pack knows all about his abuse and neglect, but none of them were willing to stand up for me or protect me.

I step to the side when he lunges, palming his large wrist and snapping it instantly, letting the knife clatter against the wood floor. He wants to shift, I can see it in his eyes, but he's too scared to defy the Alphas. He's the coward.

But I'm not. I'm not afraid of anyone anymore.

Krissy was the first to find me when the smoke went up, naked and covered in my father's blood, the metallic taste coating my tongue and cheeks.

There were moments of regret between my bouts of rage when I ripped his flesh from his bones, moments I wondered what kind of man he used to be with his brothers by his side and my mother in his arms.

I tried to be obedient my entire life, never stepping out of line. I tried to love him through his pain, even to bond with him over our shared loss, but he only had hate in his heart for me. Even in his final moments, his bitterness never wavered, and his eyes were cold and distant. It was like he'd been dead all these years already.

He spent my entire life beating me, controlling me, never being able to look into my eyes and see the parts of me that resemble my mother. But after I let my wolf take him apart, I made sure my human eyes were the last thing the miserable man saw as he drew his final breath.

Krissy couldn't convince the pack of my innocence when they found us huddled before my father's rundown home, watching the flames engulf the rickety bits of wood. I never realized the pack would care if my father died, but they saw my actions as the worst betrayal.

Killing one of your own. To them, I was no better than the shifters who chose to go against their pack and work with the hunters.

They wanted me gone before the sun was up, and their reasoning was made clear; a wolf without loyalty is of no use to the pack.

Amara and Krissy cried when I left, but I reminded Krissy of the promise I made her. I would be back one day, and I was going to make everything better for her family.

I know she trusts me, even if no one else does.

CHAPTER 6

BENJI (1821)

Over the last six years, we traveled everywhere with the circus, and I sang my heart out. We found out my sister also has a voice to please the audience, and we sing together almost every night. If not on stage, then surrounded by our new friends and family around the fire after dinner. My parents help set up and break down the circus exhibits when we move. Though it took some time, my mothers are smiling and laughing again.

My little sister has been the best friend I could ask for, and as strange as it has been to watch her grow up so quickly, she's radiant in her new life. As she pulled away to be with the other girls her age over the past year, I spent more time in my head, bantering with my wolf. She hasn't needed me to protect her the way it was when we were alone, and as I finally let my guard down, I found the company of random women and draining bottles of whiskey to be my favorite pastime.

After the long, dusty days traveling by wagon up and down the coast, I would sing to a new crowd every night we were open, and as the shadows crept over our campsite, so did the women looking for a good time. Fuck having a pack and staying in one place. This is the good life.

"Benji, get up." Zoe's voice sounds distant but stern.

"What time is it?" I groan, covering my face with the blanket.

"Time for you to wake up and take me to get a dress," she says way too excitedly for this early in the morning. We'd just gotten to town last night and set up camp, but my sister has been talking about the city dress shop for days.

"Maybe we shouldn't have drank so much last night," my wolf whines. I knew my sister would want to go shopping today, but it's been a while since she asked me to accompany her. She usually hitches a ride with Dad or Henry when they go to town to announce our arrival. If I'd known she'd want me to take her, I'd have drunk way less last night.

She shakes me again. "Alright, alright, Zoe, let me get up." I sit up, stifling a yawn.

"Give me five minutes, and then we'll go."

As soon as she leaves, I lie back down.

"Come on, we have to go," my wolf says from his sleepy corner. *"Maybe we'll meet some new ladies in town."*

An hour later, I'm out roaming the town with my sister on my arm, squinting against the harsh sun.

She's wearing one of her nicest dresses, cinched at the waist and flaring out in a wide skirt. She looks much older than sixteen, twirling a white silk parasol with the air of a woman who knows exactly what she's looking for.

"I don't see why you need a new dress for opening night tomorrow. What's wrong with the one you've got on?" She casts a scathing look at me and shakes her head.

"Tomorrow's guests are very important, and this town has

the best dress shop for miles. Why wouldn't I get something nice?"

"If I didn't know any better, Zoe, I'd think having a weekly wage has spoiled you rotten. I hope the man you marry one day knows what he's getting into."

She smiles and looks back toward the shops lining the street, her chin up and shoulders back like a real lady. "The man I intend to marry will love draping his wife in pretty things."

It takes a moment for her words to settle into my whiskey-bent brain, and I stop dead in my tracks as she continues walking without me. "The man you intend to marry? I'll be damned if you just spit marriage intentions at me casually and walk away."

She laughs as I catch up, and a dark blush creeps into her cheeks when I grab her shoulder and turn her to face me.

"Benji, you're gonna wrinkle my dress." She fusses over the fabric and tries to ignore the way I stand with my arms crossed, waiting for answers.

"Who is this man you intend to marry, Zoe, and why am I just hearing about him now?"

She twists the parasol nervously in her hands like she's wringing wet laundry to hang on the line. "It's not like he's asked me to marry him or anything. We met in the last town, and he's amazing. He didn't miss a single one of my shows, and every night he'd bring me flowers and tell me about all the places he's been with his family. I can see myself with a man like him."

"You mean a wealthy man?" She looks embarrassed and points over my shoulder at the dress shop.

"Come on, the shop's right there. We'll talk about Felix later. I just know you'll love him!"

"Felix, is it?"

She grins up at me, gathers her skirt in one fist, and takes off running, her red curls bouncing joyfully. "Beat you there," she shouts over her shoulder, and just like that, she's back to being the little girl I've missed, playfully racing through the streets as the wind carries her melodic laughter back to me and the ribbons on her dress dance behind her.

My heart aches when I think about her getting married and starting a family one day, but I've seen how the men stare at her when she's on stage. I wonder how many days, weeks, or years I have left with my little Zoe before she becomes someone else's everything.

By the time I push through the door of the designer dress shop, my sister has two older women holding different colored fabrics up to her flushed face. "Be right with you," the white-haired woman chimes.

"He's with me," my sister says, twirling around with an armful of bright pink fabric.

"So much for finding women," my wolf sighs, noticing the empty shop around us.

I find a place to sit and close my eyes, still feeling sleepy. Who knows how long this is going to take? Just as I'm dozing off, a soft voice startles me awake.

"Can I get you anything?" I open my eyes, taking in the young woman standing before me with a flirty smile.

I grin, leaning forward in my chair, and her back arches, pushing her breasts in front of my face. *"Now this is more like it,"* my wolf practically leaps to his feet.

I open my mouth to talk to the pretty lady when my sister calls out, "Benji, love, what do you think about this color?" The pretty girl's face falls when she assumes my sister is my wife. Before I can set the record straight, the girl turns quickly and begins hanging new dresses in the store window, clearly embarrassed.

"She's my sister," I hiss over my shoulder, hoping the gorgeous girl in the window will come back and give me another shot. One of the older ladies brings a roll of emerald-green fabric to me, waiting for my approval.

"I think it will look beautiful," I tell her, knowing it will compliment her pale skin and red hair.

"How long do you think it would take to fashion a dress from this?" she asks hopefully.

The lady beams at my sister and calls to the young woman up front. "Charlotte, can you fetch the pretty green dress in the back for me? The one I made for the Prescot girl who changed her mind?"

"Charlotte, that's a pretty name," I tell her, but she only glances at me briefly as she passes, and I feel my frustration rising. Zoe covers a laugh with the back of her hand, and I scowl across the shop, knowing how much joy it brings her to warn off a potential one-night stand.

"Is this the one, grandma?" Charlotte brings the dress to the older shopkeeper, and my sister nearly squeals in delight.

"I think this one was meant for a pretty redhead like you," she tells Zoe. "I can take your measurements and have it ready for you tomorrow." The lady grabs the roll of fabric from my sister and replaces it with the beautiful dress with puffy sleeves.

Charlotte stands so close that I can brush my finger over one of her slender arms, and when she drags her hopeful smile back to me, my sister can't help herself.

"Oh, tomorrow will be perfect! Benji is taking me to the circus in town for our anniversary!" Charlotte scoffs and takes off toward the back room, mumbling something about me being a lying scoundrel. The older woman smiles from ear to ear as she lathers my sister with attention and takes her measurements.

Zoe refuses to meet my angry stare, but I know she hears me when I tell her I'm gonna get her back for this. Her face falls as if she hadn't thought about my retaliation.

Last night, I got drunk after my performance, and three women claiming to be best friends crawled into my tent with me. Most of it was a blur, but the things they were willing to do made getting turned down by Charlotte at the dress shop a far-off memory.

"Benji!" my sister shouts, moving me back and forth. I groan, not wanting to open my eyes.

"She's too loud," my wolf says, trying to cover his ears with his paws.

"I know. I hope she leaves." I open one eye and then the other. Judging by her flared nostrils and narrowed eyes, I'd say she's been trying to wake me for a while. Either that, or she saw the three women crawling out of my tent this morning.

It's confirmed when she opens her mouth to talk. "Benji, I've been trying to get you up for the past thirty minutes. We were supposed to get my dress an hour ago." Her brows dip low in a frown.

"You said you wouldn't drink last night and would be up early to take me. Now we're late, and I still have to fix my hair."

"Sorry, Zoe," I say, actually feeling bad about it. She's been talking about this day nonstop. "What's so important about these people coming tonight?"

She turns away as if hiding her reaction from me. "It's nothing, Benji."

"Is it about that guy you were talking about yesterday?" I throw it out there since it's the first thing that comes to mind. I don't believe it, but judging by her wide eyes, I assumed right.

"Yes, okay, you win. Felix promised he would be here tonight with his family. He said it will be my most special performance yet. I just didn't want to give you the time to come up with some way to embarrass me."

My wolf wants to growl, but I shut my lips tightly. I want her to trust me, but I'm angry at myself for not seeing this sooner.

"He uh—" she smiles slowly, and I want to know every-thing there is to know about this guy. "He's really important to me, Benji. I think he's the one for me."

"So his family is loaded, and that's why you needed a new dress?" I try not to show any emotion on the outside, but I know what sort of men come here with their families, and my alarms are going off.

"Yeah," she says in a small voice. Suddenly I'm inter-ested in this show tonight. "I just want his family to like me too."

"Is he human?" *Please let him be supernatural,* I repeat over and over to myself.

"He's human." She cringes as she waits for my reaction. *Shit.*

"Does he know what we are?" I ask slowly and carefully, knowing the rules very well about keeping ourselves hidden.

"No!" She shakes her head vigorously. "I didn't tell him. I wouldn't."

A part of me is relieved she hasn't let our secret slip, but I know it's not realistic for her to marry a human and spend her life in their world as if her wolf isn't a huge part of who she is.

"I'll tell you what." She looks at me again. "How about you fix your hair in all those springy curls you like so much, and I will pick up your dress for you."

"Really?" she asks, and I nod my head. Overjoyed, she leans in to hug me and kiss me on the forehead. "This isn't just so you can talk to that woman at the dress shop without me, is it?" She pulls back and watches my face skeptically.

"If it is, you'll never know." She punches my shoulder and shakes her head, but even my whore ways can't wipe the excitement from her face.

Once I'm dressed, I make my way out of our campground toward the tent where the animals are kept. I saddle up the fastest horse we have to make the ride into town, knowing a wagon would only slow me down.

"So, sister has a boyfriend, huh?" my wolf says, poking his head out from the corner of his cave.

"Yeah, it seems like it," I respond.

"Can't wait to meet him," he says, baring his teeth.

"Yeah, me too."

When I finally make it to the shop, the same white-haired woman from yesterday smiles wide and disappears into the back to get my sister's dress. While I wait for her to return, I pace the store, looking for the pretty granddaughter to invite to our show tonight and maybe to my tent after.

The grandma comes back quickly and hands me the delicate green dress, and though I am disappointed not seeing Charlotte, I'm anxious to get back to camp and meet this mystery man my sister is so excited to see.

Before I get to our campground, I immediately stop. My heart thumps loudly, overpowering my senses. I breathe in to calm myself.

Something isn't right. My instincts tell me to run, but if something is wrong, my family will need me. I grip my sister's dress and make my way to the camp.

Everything is still—too quiet.

"This is strange."

I slide off the back of the horse and walk the grassy field, touching a tree stump when I spot blood splattering the bark. My palms grow sweaty as I walk around a bush and spot the body of a female Faerie dead on the ground. My stomach rocks like a ship at sea, but I keep moving toward camp quietly.

Bodies litter the grass and woods as if they'd been attacked while trying to run away. My pulse quickens, and I move faster to check in on my parents and sister. I can't look down into the ashen faces of the friends and family I'd grown to know and love.

What happened?

This is a massacre. I was gone for less than an hour.

Sweat beads down my brow. I want to yell, but whoever did this might still be around. When I get close to my parents' tent, I hear voices and pause.

"Where's the boy?" A man demands in a grating tone.

"This is all of them . . . my family." My father's fear-laced voice quivers. My body starts to shake. I'm going to puke. "You've killed all of them . . . taken my little girl from me."

My breath leaves my body, and I collapse to my knees. My mothers, my baby Zoe, all of them were gone in a second. I want to scream at the unfairness of it all. I should have been here to protect them, to protect my sister like I always have. I knew better than to assume there is safety in numbers after the last home we lost.

I'd rather be dead by her side than alive knowing I failed

her. I told her to stay here. If I had taken her with me . . . What am I going to do without them?

Someone touches my shoulder, and I immediately flinch, turning to see Henry covered in blood.

"Go," he says in a weak voice. Leave before they find you. Your dad's giving you a chance to escape. Take it and go," he pleads.

"Who did this?" I whisper. My already broken heart shatters into a million pieces.

He gives me a grave look and I know without being told.

"Hunters," I say with disgust.

"Kill him," the same voice says before my dad screams and then abruptly goes silent. I swallow hard when a loud thump hits the ground, and I know he's gone too.

"Is that her, Felix?" No! My breathing picks up, I think I'm going to have a panic attack.

My sister was dating a guy named Felix. She'd gotten a new dress for him and was taking the time to curl her hair because she cared about what he thought of her. She was brimming with excitement to meet the guy's family tonight, and he turned on her. She was quietly waiting for him to propose when she turned eighteen, waiting for everything she'd dreamed of, but instead, he cost her everything.

"Yeah, that's her, but Zoe said she had a brother. I'm not sure if we got him already." The young voice responds, and rage sets fire to my insides. How fucking dare he say her name so casually while she's lying dead on the ground . . . killed while she fussed over her hair to impress him.

My heart breaks. I want to go in there and see my family, to rip the heads off the men that murdered them, but my dad bought me time, and I do the hardest thing I've ever done in my life.

I run.

I find the horse mulling the field with my sister's dress draped over the saddle, and I take off.

I'm a coward for running, but I also don't want my dad's sacrifice to be meaningless. I'm not sure where I'm headed, but I know one thing, I can't stay here anymore.

CHAPTER 7

BENJI (1822)

I t's been a year since I lost my family. The grief is always there, but it becomes a living, breathing part of me that my wolf and I shoulder alone. The nightmares are less frequent now, but I doubt I'll ever be free from the sound of my father's last scream or the memories of my sassy little sister dancing around on stage with me.

Just as I finish singing my set, I smell the scent of a vampire tangled in the earthy aroma of the tavern. My eyes land on the man headed toward me. He stands out like a shiny new cent lying in the muck as he drifts through the sweaty crowd of drunks with beer sloshing over the tops of their glasses.

I'm wary, but not because he's a vampire—I'm used to different supernaturals. He's not dressed like the usual patrons of this establishment; he looks expensive.

"Benjamin," he says with a smile that has my hackles rising. No one has called me that since my family died. "My name is Silas, and I work with the council."

Council? What the fuck do they want with me?

"I'm deeply sorry for your loss." He waits a moment to

see if I'll say something, but I have nothing to say. "I'd like to make you an offer." I don't like where this is going. I look around to see if anyone has noticed this man, but everyone is already drunk. "Come work for us."

I drag my eyes over to his as he follows me to an empty table in a dark corner. "What makes you think I want to work for you guys?"

"Well, for starters, you have no family. Your pack wants your head. If you come to work for us, we'll make sure they won't lay a hand on you, and we'll give you a purpose."

Purpose? Do I really want one?

I was content traveling from town to town, singing and drinking, but now—I'm not so sure.

"Leave me alone," I finally say. "I want nothing to do with you."

He chuckles. "How about I offer you a way to avenge your family's death?" Even my wolf gets up from his lazy position on the floor.

"How do you know about that?" I grip my glass tighter, surprised it doesn't break inside my grip.

"He better not be working with the hunters," my wolf says, pacing back and forth on edge.

"The council knows everything going on with the supernatural community." I don't know if those words are to scare me, but my vision turns red in anger. It's almost as if I'm reliving that moment all over again. Listening to my father scream his last scream over the dead bodies of my sister and mothers.

He's got my full attention now.

"Why didn't you guys stop it?" I spit through gritted teeth. My wolf is ready to pounce, but I'm keeping him at bay.

I slam both fists down on the wobbly table when he

doesn't respond quickly, then glance around the tavern at the heads turning in our direction.

I lower my voice. "If the almighty council knew what was happening, why didn't you do shit to protect my family?" They've got people who do the dirty jobs for them. Why didn't they just send those supes to help?

"I'm sorry we weren't there on time, but we can offer you money, along with the chance to kill the people who did this to your family."

My heartbeat rages as my wolf paces back and forth, growling with pent-up frustration. I don't consider us violent, but when you lose your whole family to hunters, you lose a piece of yourself you can never get back.

"How will you offer me that?" This time I grab my beer and finish the whole glass.

"It's simple." He slides a piece of paper across the table, leaving it there. It takes me a moment before I pick it up and open it.

"What's this?"

He grins, showing me his sharp fangs. "These are the coordinates to the hunters who set up the raid that killed your family."

I run my thumb through the perfectly written numbers before answering, "What do you want for this information?" There has to be a reason he gave me this. The council always has its own agenda.

"Nothing, it's a gift." He sits back on his chair, relaxed as if we're old friends catching up over a beer.

I don't completely trust this guy, but how can I turn down this information? I've wanted their heads ever since the massacre that destroyed my first pack, but instead of hunting them down, I got comfortable living our lives with the circus, drinking myself stupid, running around with women, singing, and acting like they weren't still out there looking for us. I laid my guard down, and they crept back in and took everything I loved.

He puts his hands on the table, pushing himself up to leave, but not before saying, "I look forward to seeing how you destroy them."

I watch as he walks out the door, then I order another drink and tell the barkeep to keep them coming.

It takes three days to find the location Silas gave me, but I have to be sure these are the right people. There were dozens of them the night my pack was burned to the ground, but I've only seen four men coming and going. The blood of four hunters doesn't feel like it could ever be enough to ease my suffering.

After a year of dreaming of all the ways to avenge my family's death, this is it.

I've hidden in the brush surrounding their dilapidated barn all week, watching who comes and goes every day. There's an older man with silver hair who looks to be calling the shots, and three younger men scramble to haul in a load of weapons from a nearby covered wagon.

"Dad, we are wasting time here. There's enough black powder to make sure their pack doesn't make it out of the flames. The whole place will go up in minutes." The youngest of the men slings a crossbow over his shoulder and picks up a crate to haul inside.

"Felix, we stick to the plan. That's how this works. Shit gets messy when you go in blind." My blood runs cold. That name triggers a memory of Zoe on the last day I spent with her, twirling her parasol over her shoulder and blushing when she said, *Felix.*

Every time I've heard the name in passing over the last year, my body freezes, and I hold my breath, wondering if it's the same man my sister spoke of. I never saw his face the day he slayed my family, but I will never forget their voices. I hear them every time I close my eyes at night.

Felix walks into the house to dump his load and comes back, glaring at his dad. "Travis and Pete think we can take them by ourselves. There aren't a lot of them."

"We make a plan and stick to it. Pete and Travis are trying to get you killed," the older man says, raising his voice loud enough to carry to the other two hunters in the house.

Felix drags two more crossbows from the wagon, mumbling under his breath and shooting glances over his shoulder. "But Dad, if we don't go now, we might lose the chance. The girl said they're going to be leaving soon."

"Enough, Felix," the man shouts, his tone sending a wave of nausea rolling through me. The same tone he used when he ordered my father's death.

I squeeze my eyes, trying to get the memory out of my head, but I can't do anything about it. It's ingrained there and will live with me for the rest of my life. "We'll take you to the edge of their property tonight so you can wait for that stupid girl again when she does her rounds. You'll convince her to keep her family right where they are. I don't care what you have to do."

Bile rises in my throat as I picture Zoe again. She was the girl Felix used before. She was how they tracked us and knew everything about us. Now he's using some other young shifter to do the same thing.

The men Felix referred to as Travis and Pete are trading underhanded looks as they disappear into the house with the last load of weapons. I have no clue who they are, but I know one thing—they're all going down. I'm not leaving anyone alive.

They leave for two hours every night. I assume they're using Felix to infiltrate another pack and earn their trust, and as they load into their covered wagon, I see a faint light flickering through the window of their house.

Idiots.

I'm not sure what my plan is when I push through the unlocked door, but I find crates filled with glass jars of alcohol and an arsenal of rifles, bows, knives, and barrels of black powder.

The kid's words come to mind as I kick the biggest barrel over and watch the sooty substance slide over the floor like sand.

"There's enough black powder to make sure their pack doesn't make it out of the flames. The whole place will go up in minutes."

"Looks like they like fire," I tell my wolf, chuckling to myself as I search the house for everything I need. After kicking over the barrels of powder, smashing jars of alcohol, and pocketing a few more of their fancy toys, I know exactly how to draw them out. The low flickering oil lamp in their kitchen will do just fine.

There are stacks of hay I've been sleeping on in the abandoned barn in the woods, and after hauling some to the back porch and making an oil-soaked trail to their kitchen, I can hardly wait for them to return.

When I hear the wagon clunking along the dirt road in the distance, I know this is it. My body trembles with excitement.

I hear them laughing at a young girl's expense, talking about the crude, awful things they should do to her once they burn her family's home to the ground. The old man seems proud of Felix.

I drop the oil lamp into the trail of hay and watch as the oil catches and burns the back porch quickly, hypnotized by the dancing flames. Excitement shoots through me, and I take off into the woods to circle the property.

They're walking into a dark house now, wondering what wild animal or trespasser could have possibly caused so much damage. Their voices are angry, blaming each other, not paying attention to the heat and the smell carrying through the back of the house.

Finally, the flames ignite the black powder on the kitchen floor, and the whole back of the house seems to explode with huge coils of flames and clouds of smoke.

This is how they burned my pack's home and fields so quickly. I've never seen flames so big, but I stare into them, completely mesmerized. It makes sense how easily someone could get obsessed with setting things on fire and blowing them up.

I draw the rifle over my shoulder and aim for the front door, my eyes never wavering from the house.

The men scream, and my wolf and I smile.

The front door swings open, but only the old man and Felix are crawling out on their bellies, trying not to inhale the smoke, and looking like the snakes they are.

They're coughing and choking as they tumble down the steps and into the fresh air. The coppery smell of blood hits me as I move forward. Shards of glass from broken jars pierced their forearms where they crawled through the mess I made.

My wolf licks his lips at the sight.

The other two men don't make it out, and their screams

go silent as the hungry flames devour the entire house in minutes—just like Felix promised.

The older man sees me first, approaching with my stolen rifle pointed at his son's head.

"Stand up." He eyes me up and down, weighing his odds of being able to tackle me and take me out, but I lay the barrel flush against his son's temple and grit my teeth. "Stand. Up."

He does what he's told as Felix whimpers and squirms against the gun's barrel. As soon the old man stands, shoulders back, pride in his dark eyes, I tip the rifle toward his knees and blow them out from under him.

His howls of pain are magic, sending goosebumps rippling across my skin. "Sorry about that," I say. "Just wanted to make sure you got a front-row seat for the show. My little sister wanted to make a good impression on the family of her suitor, after all. It's just a shame she can't be here for my best performance yet."

Recognition flickers in Felix's eyes, and I know without a doubt that these are the right men.

The father seems preoccupied with his injury and trying to stop the bleeding, but his attention shifts to us when I grip his son's neck and lift him off his feet.

I lift him into the air, looking into the eyes of the man Zoe was so captured by. He weighs nothing compared to my strength.

I toss my gun off into the bushes and let my claws break from my skin with a smile.

"Please, don't. I'll do anything, please," he begs.

I hold the boy closer to my face as I whisper, "Did Zoe beg you before you killed her? Did you look her in the eyes, make her watch her mothers die first?"

"I . . . I didn't. I . . . they—" he stutters wildly, unable to find the right words, but I push through his flesh and bones to silence him, grab his heart, and rip it out of his chest. Much like the way he and his family ripped my heart out a year ago.

He falls to the ground, the noise echoing through the stillness of the forest.

The old man can't take his eyes off his dead son in front of him.

"You killed a lot of innocent people," I growl, stooping in front of him and wiping his son's blood onto the front of his shirt with slow, agonizing movements.

"They're evil. They deserved to die," he spits like the words leave a bad taste in his mouth.

"We never did anything to you guys. You're the ones who killed the kindest supes I've ever met." My heart breaks for every single one of them.

"Your sister deserved to die." My body freezes, anger roiling through my body. "Zoe wasn't normal."

All I see is red.

The next thing I know, he's on the ground, decapitated. I'm not sure when I reacted; I just blacked out.

"Well, well, well." It looks like they got what was coming to them." The dark look in his ruby red eyes tells me this was a test, and I passed.

I watch as Silas looks at the dead body with glee. "I knew you had it in you. The fire was a nice touch."

"Did you follow me?" How long has he been here? How did I not smell his scent?

He looks around the forest before he answers me. "I had to see if you'd actually do it."

I'm not sure what to say. I finally got revenge for my family's death, but it still doesn't bring them back or fix the ache inside me. There's still an empty hole in my chest.

"What do you say, Benji? Can I count on you to join us?" When I stay silent he continues, "You'll get to kill a lot more hunters and protect families like yours before they get destroyed."

It's like he can read my soul. I don't want any other supe to go through what I just went through.

There is only one response to give.

"Yes."

CHAPTER 8

ASH (1822)

Hopping from pack to pack isn't what I expected. I was hoping to find the perfect fit for me, but so far, I've traveled to seven packs over the last four years, and I've hated them all.

None of them feel like home, and once they get a sense of my power, they want me even less. The Alphas are afraid I'll threaten their power, and they're right. As soon as I find a pack I like, I'm taking it over as my own.

"We'll find our place," my wolf says, encouraging me to keep going. *"Until then, you have me,"* he says, and I snort when he shows me his teeth.

The spring breeze assaults my nose as I make my way down a cobblestone street, looking down alleyways and in shop windows for something to occupy my time. A different scent hits me as the wind sweeps in a new direction—another *shifter?* This is strange; they're usually not this close to humans.

I come around the corner as a thin, blond man slams someone against a brick wall, and I watch the scene unfold with interest.

"Leave me alone," the sniveling man against the wall pleads. He looks like he was plucked straight from his bed, dressed in silk night clothes and a look of utter confusion.

"My how the tables have turned." The blond man holding him in place has a cold, shrill voice, so dark and void of emotion. "Now you know what it feels like, don't you? Tell me, how do you like begging for a change?"

Taking in the shifter's hollow cheeks and baggy, frayed clothes, I wonder if he's a rogue. They live on the street and kill with no remorse.

"You always loved to make me beg for mercy." The young blond shifter shoves the older guy to his knees in the alley, and I can smell the fear wafting off him. I feel like I should help the man, and send this irate shifter on his way, but I'm frozen in place as his words wash over me.

"You think those other children didn't deserve to control what happened to their bodies? They pleaded for you to stop too, but did you?"

"I don't . . . I don't know what you're talking about," he stutters, and his lie only makes the blond tighten his grip.

"I recognized the sound of your shoes striking the ground and the pitch of your nasal voice. I can still smell the brothel on your clothes and skin for fuck's sake. I know who you are. I've been hunting you for six fucking years. Do you really think I wouldn't remember you and all your fucked-up demands?"

"I don't know what you're talking about!"

"Really?" the blond says with a harsh laugh. "So, paying Hank to spend time with boys he kidnapped off the street so you could tie them up, whip them, beat them, rape them . . . That doesn't ring a bell?" He tightens his fist around the man's clothing.

Now that I know the person is scum, I turn around to walk

away, leaving the shifter to do whatever he wants to the human.

"Wait," my wolf growls.

I listen to what's going on. It's silent until I hear a fist meeting someone's flesh, and I know that's the wolf.

"Leave him alone!" Someone else shouts. There's a fearful quiver to the new man's voice, but he's trying to sound tough.

"You're something evil," the man on the ground says through a mouthful of loose teeth.

"I might be something different than what you are, but let's be clear, we're both *evil*."

More footsteps echo down the alley, and I make my way back to the scene only to find three more people gathered around the shifter. It looks like I came back just in time.

The shifter drops the piece of shit to the ground as he steps back and turns into a wolf. He's ruthless in the way he claws at the man trying to crawl away from him, almost like he's putting on a show for the three bystanders.

He could end all their lives quickly, but he smells excited like he's dying for a challenge.

When his victim falls into a silent and motionless heap on the ground, he turns for the other three watching in horror. It's almost funny how he gives them a moment to gather their thoughts, and when they lunge for him, he snatches the heavyset one up like a cat toying with a mouse.

With one massive paw to the big man's throat, he leans in for the kill, but both his friends leap onto his back, trying their best to choke the wolf.

"Fuck it. We've got nothing else to do." My wolf leaps to the front of my mind as I run to help my fellow shifter. My claws burst from my fingertips, and I take down the one closest to me, ripping through his spine and grabbing his

heart. He falls with a loud thump. The one in front of me looks at his friend lying on the grass before looking back at me. His eyes widen in fear when he sees the talons coming from my fingertips. Whatever he told himself to explain the wolf in front of him has clearly gone out the window now that there are two of us.

Before he can say anything, a knife goes right through his throat, and blood pours from his mouth as he goes down.

The blond man turns his hard gaze on me, no longer in wolf form, and instead of looking appreciative like I thought he would, he's got a scowl on his face.

"You ruined my fun," he says in a bored tone as I shift back into human form, keeping an eye on the bloody knife he's twirling to make sure he won't try to use it against me.

"I thought you'd be grateful." I stand a little straighter to let him know he doesn't intimidate me one bit, and I watch him do the same. He's a strong one, probably an Alpha just like me. I have to be extra careful, though it's very rare, some shifters have powers. I don't want to be caught off guard.

He assesses me with his wolf eyes, and I do the same.

Deciding he's not a threat, I search the bodies on the ground for the person with the least amount of blood on their clothes and start undressing him. The blond man does the same, eyeing me suspiciously. as we both get dressed. I start to introduce myself, but a noise stops us both abruptly. Footsteps. Unnaturally fast footsteps.

"Hunters," I say, watching his brows furrow. "We have to get out of here."

We stare at each other for a moment before taking off at full speed. He's the first wolf I've ever met who looked confused by hunters. What world has he been living in while these groups of men terrorize our people?

CHAPTER 9

AZ (1822)

I'm sprinting to lose the hunters tailing me. I'd planned this little endeavor of mine to be late at night when most humans are fast asleep. I've spent six long years roaming the streets, meeting random shifters, learning about what I am, and hunting down the violent man from the brothel who made my life a living hell.

I wanted the satisfaction of pulling the slimy bastard out of his comfortable bed. I needed to invade his space, show him what it feels like to scream, and have no one give a fuck. His shitty friends were just a bonus.

Those bastards deserved a fate far worse than the death they received.

But the shifter in the alley came out of nowhere, and until now, I've been on my own. It would be easier if I could find others like me for protection, but I'm sure I'm too damaged for anyone to want to take me in.

I'm not a good man.

The men who paid to hurt children were bloodthirsty, and they tormented me until I broke. Now I live for the same crimson life force they drew from my body night after night. I live for the hunt, the kill, the sweet trickle of warm blood flowing through my fingertips. I'm obsessed, and I know this can't be normal, even for a wolf shifter.

As soon as this other wolf realizes how fucked up I am, he'll be gone too. That's if he doesn't decide to put me out of my misery first.

I've spent most of my nights on the streets, in and out of taverns, but no matter how much I drink, I never feel buzzed. The women fall at my feet in droves for some reason, and though I thought I'd never want to be touched again, I find the sight and feel of blood dripping down a woman's soft curves to be the only thing capable of getting me hard.

There's only one difference between the man who stood over me with his whip and the man I have become.

I ask for permission.

I make sure the women know exactly what I want from them, and if they aren't eager to please, I would never force them the way I've been forced.

In the distance, the shifter's pale hair stands out like a torch as we stick to the shadows. Our clothing was left in tattered piles back in the alleyway, but I managed to grab my knife before we took off.

I'm used to looking out for myself, not anyone else, and it has worked well so far. But something inside me pulls my body toward the other shifter, racing after him as if my life depends on it.

Two sets of footsteps are hot on my trail. I don't know how many hunters there were or what they will do if they catch me, but I know I need to take them down before more follow.

I come to a complete stop and hide behind a tree as I wait for them to catch up to me. I lost sight of the other shifter, but running forever isn't an option.

"Let's play," my wolf says, and I grin, twirling my knife around my fingers.

The adrenaline pumps through me as I wait for the two hunters to approach me, but it seems strange how long they're taking to catch up. They should have passed me by now.

I move my neck just a bit, but I don't see anything.

"What the fuck is taking them so long?" My wolf is impatient, already wanting more blood.

"I don't know. Maybe they're hiding too."

A few minutes pass, and when I still don't hear footsteps, I know something isn't right. I brace myself, leave my post, and quietly walk until the two motionless bodies on the ground catch my attention.

Dead hunters, lying with their mouths agape.

"You're welcome . . . again." A cocky voice from the shadows nearly scares the shit out of me. I'll never admit it to anyone, though. That's the second time he's caught me off guard, and I don't like it.

I compose myself quickly before turning around to glare at the white-haired shifter. "Those were my kills," I growl.

I set my eyes on him, ready to attack if he tries anything, when a voice demands my attention.

"Gentlemen."

I follow the cold voice of a well-dressed man. He smiles, but it's not friendly. I back up until I'm right next to the white-haired shifter.

"I saw you kill those humans in town, and it was a sight to see," he says with a dreamy sigh.

I don't like this one bit. How did I not know he was there?

"And you, Ash, the way you killed all those hunters and never lost a breath. That was beautiful," he says, and I watch as he smiles, revealing the tips of fangs protruding from his mouth.

I keep twirling my knife, waiting impatiently to see what this newcomer will do. "Ah, my apologies for not introducing myself. My name is Silas, and I'm part of the council."

I'm even more confused now. "What the hell is the council, and what do you want with us?"

"I'm here with an offer." He tosses an open pack at our feet and slides one hand into his pocket. "First, help yourself to whatever you need in there." He nods at the bag the other shifter has scooped up, but I don't take my eyes off Silas.

The white-haired guy raises his brow as he begins to sift through the food inside the man's pack. "What's the offer?" he asks skeptically.

"We want blood. We should kill the vampire," my wolf says as he assesses the man in front of us. I take a deep breath to calm myself.

"The council wants you to come work for us."

"I don't know if I like this," my wolf voices.

The last time I was offered a job by a strange man in town, it didn't turn out the way he'd promised.

"And you, Aziel, I know how bloodthirsty you are. You will never run out of assignments. You can kill as much as you want."

My body tenses when my name falls from his lips. It's the first time I've heard it out loud since I left the brothel, and I try not to picture the way the men used to spit my name from their filthy mouths as they barked commands.

"Ash, you'll have a place to stay, and you won't have to worry about looking for a pack. You'll have somewhere to belong where your father's name has never been uttered."

I look at the man called Ash, but he turns his face into the shadows.

"You'll have all the money you could ever hope for, boys." I've never had any before, and I can tell from the way Ash's eyes focus on the man, he hasn't either. The idea of being able to buy property is enticing. I've never owned anything before.

"I'll do it," I say as Ash nods silently beside me in agreement. I only hope I'm not making another huge mistake.

CHAPTER 10

TYLER (1822)

It's the end of my last year at Mystic Shadow Academy. I beat everyone in my class in all aspects except for magic because uh . . . well . . . I don't have any.

"We would've been at the top too if we were born witches," my wolf reminds me.

But, I'm still not satisfied. I've been trained by my dads and my mom, and everything was easier here than compared to home. I think my fathers made sure I was over-prepared.

"Tyler!" Fuck, Owen found me again. The three other Betas found their mate in their second year of college. She was a transfer, and though she is beautiful, she isn't mine. I always knew I wasn't meant to be a part of their pack, but now my fathers and the other Betas are lost about what to do with me. Their plans have unraveled, and they constantly argue over what I'm supposed to do now.

I don't belong with them. They can take over as Betas if my parents retire or goddess forbid something happens to them.

I try walking faster and ignoring Owen. I've been trying to avoid him and the other Betas for the past four years, but now that we all know I'm not mated to the same girl, I don't have to be polite or pretend to give a fuck when they find me. I hated them when we lived together as a pack, and I still hate them now. They didn't grow on me like my mom said they would.

"What does he want now?" My wolf gets up from his nap, clearly annoyed by Owen's presence. *"They have nothing to do with us anymore since we're not part of their little group."* My wolf is wounded, being the only one in the group to not find our mate.

He grabs my shoulder as I quickly turn around, pinning him to the wall with my arm. "Don't ever touch me," I growl, my vision sharpening and changing as my wolf emerges.

His eyes shift to amber, ready for a fight just like me. "Don't, Owen." Brandon pulls him back. "It's not worth it."

Owen releases me as his eyes go back to normal, but I'm still looking through the eyes of my wolf.

"I'm so happy to be graduating tomorrow." I let out an exasperated sigh.

"What are we doing after?" My wolf narrows his eyes as we watch them leave.

When they're out of sight, I start to relax. *"I don't know, wolf. I don't know."*

That's the truth. We don't fit in anywhere. My whole life consisted of training to take over my parents' position, and now the opportunity has been taken away.

I didn't train my whole life and become the top of my class only to work as a blacksmith with The Nightshade Growlers.

It's been rough since I came back from the academy. I

don't know where I belong, and I'm more confused now than I've ever been.

I've tried hundreds of jobs within this pack, but nothing satisfies me.

I'm so out of place, but I just don't know where to go. It doesn't help to see Owen, Dylan, and Brandon home with their mate. I was so relieved when I found out I wouldn't have to be a part of their group, but now the relief has been replaced with jealousy.

They have things so easy with everything planned out for them. They don't have to wonder about their place here or in life.

My mother senses my distress and says, "Tyler, you'll find your place." I put the crate on the table before looking at her again. "You're my son, and I always know what you're thinking. Now pass me a spoon." I go to the drawer and grab it for her, wondering if it's my thoughts on my face that she can read so well.

It's Saturday morning, and I have nowhere to go. I have no friends; the only interaction I have is with my family. My brother's still in college, which means I have no one to talk to. I wish the school wasn't so far. Even in wolf form, the travel is rough, and I miss him so much. I wish there were some way to talk to him.

Lately, it feels like I never have a moment to myself, even if I did want to take off to the academy to visit my brother.

I go back to the table and grab the basket of fresh eggs I collected from the coup this morning. "Have you noticed my dads acting weird lately?" They had to go out on pack business this weekend, but they've been on my ass ever since I came back. "They're almost overbearing," I tell her, remembering last night when I tried to go out, and they all wanted to go out with me. I feel like a child who needs constant supervision.

My mom gives me a warm smile before turning around. "They just want to make sure you don't feel alone. We're your parents, after all." She cracks six eggs, pours them into a bowl, and mixes them with the spoon.

"Yeah, but they haven't left my side since I've been back. They even come along when I try out new jobs for the pack. It's kind of embarrassing." I grab the closest chair to me and sit, resting my elbows on the table.

"Maybe they just want to make sure you get treated fairly by the rest of the wolves," she says as she pours the mixture into the pan.

"Mom, everyone knows I'm your son. Everyone knew I was supposed to become a Beta." Even though I didn't want the position, I'm slightly embarrassed about the matter being out of my hands. I wanted to turn down the position on my own terms and not because the other Betas found their mate without me.

"Here you go." My mom places my breakfast of scrambled eggs and bacon in front of me.

"Thanks, Mom," I say, already digging into my food.

"I have to go to Lucile's today to pick up my dress." She takes a bite of her food.

"I'll come with you," I pipe up with the possibility of getting out of pack lands for a little while.

She almost drops her fork and looks intently at her plate. "Oh, actually, there is work that needs to be done here. I'll show you when you're finished eating."

I was looking forward to the fresh air and getting away from the pack for a while. "Yeah, okay," I agree, hanging my head over my plate.

It's already late in the evening. I didn't think Mom would have me working all day, but I guess she needs my help since my dads are out.

I finish eating my dinner and go to my room. After a few hours, my wolf is restless and so am I.

"I need to get out." My wolf paces back and forth.

"Me too." I get up from my bed and make my way downstairs.

"Mom," I call out but get no answer. She's probably already sleeping.

I open and close the door softly to avoid waking her. If she hears me leaving, she's going to get weird again and try to come with me. I've been dying for a run by myself, and as I near the edge of our property, I take a deep breath and let it out.

Finally! I get to run by myself. I have so many pent-up emotions. I'm frustrated, angry, sad, and lost.

I'm in the middle of undressing and eyeing the stretch of land before me when light footsteps sound behind me. I quickly turn toward the noise, expecting my mom to be there with another excuse for why I can't go out on my own.

"Tyler," A smooth voice calls out.

A strange man stands before me with pale skin and bright red eyes, and when the wind shifts, I smell his familiar stench. He's a vampire. "Can I help you?"

"What the fuck does this guy want. He's ruining our time." My wolf paces again.

"It's what I can do to help you." He's got a knowing glint in his eye.

"Look, man, I'm not in the mood. If you have something to say just spill it. I don't have time for this shit." I came here to decompress, not to fight, although a fight doesn't sound half bad.

"My name is Silas, and I'm with the council. It's been very hard to reach you. Your family has been glued to your side at every turn." Now I'm intrigued. "You don't belong here, Tyler, but I think you already know that."

My wolf rolls his eyes as I try not to laugh.

"So what do you want, Silas?" I take a step closer to him. I'm not afraid of a brawl, and if that's what he came for, I'll give it to him. If my family has been trying to keep this guy from me, there has to be a good reason.

"If you come to work for us, you'll have a place to belong. We can use your skills to protect our supernatural community. You'll have lots of money and can start a new life wherever you want."

This deal sounds too good to be true. "What do I have to do for you guys?"

"You kill whoever harms our supernatural community. We'll send you on missions all around the world." A feeling low in my gut says it's something more than that, but I'm at the point where I need to leave this place. I can't stand another day of the Betas living their lives as if I don't exist and my parents obsessing over everything I do.

"What do you say, Tyler?" His red eyes almost look like they're glowing. He licks his lips in anticipation as he waits for my response.

I rub my chin before answering, "Sure, I'll do it." His smirk twists, and I wonder if I made the right decision.

Chapter 11

Az (1822)

I watch every single supernatural being here, knowing I can't trust anyone. They stare openly, sizing up one another. Our living quarters sleep all two hundred of us, stacked in floor-to-ceiling bunks in straight rows.

We've been here for two days. I try to remember why I even agreed to this. When the biggest of them all, a lion shifter, sneers at me. Oh yeah, the promise of money and killing. Two things I crave the most in life.

"Don't fucking touch my shit," the redhead they call Benjamin growls, and I look back at him.

That fucker is annoying as shit. He's always singing and eyeing us all with distrust. He should have joined the circus instead of coming here. I can't wait to make him bleed.

Out of all of them, I stay close to Ash. It's not like I trust him, but I can tell he and I are the same—always vigilant and ready for a fight.

"I didn't. You're the one who left your *shit* in my bed," the rich motherfucker answers. I wonder what made him want to come here. He strolled right in like he owned the place with his fine clothing and jewelry.

I lay on my bed, propped against a flat pillow, watching them argue while I play with my knife. We were all searched for weapons when we arrived, but the moment the guy was distracted by another wolf refusing to give up his pistol, I swiped my knife back from the table and rushed through.

The rich guy faces Benjamin as the crowd starts chanting, "Fight, fight, fight." Personally, my money is on the rich boy. Tyler, I think that's his name. He looks buffer than Benjamin. I'm not even sure why they brought the singer here. He doesn't belong, neither of them do, but at least I can see why the council wanted Tyler. We haven't started our training yet, but he's already shown a lot of skill.

"Everyone to your bunks, now," our leader, Tom, shouts from the door as he walks in, disbanding the crowd and their shouting.

He's a coyote shifter, and his silent partner, Theodore, stands at his back, an odd darkness around him, but I can't seem to pinpoint his intentions. He hasn't said a word yet, but he carries himself with an air of danger.

"There are two hundred of you, but only half will make it." He looks at each of us pointedly. "You work for us. Your lives are ours now."

I put my knife away, but not before imagining myself killing him slowly with a million tiny cuts.

"Everyone get to sleep." We all look briefly at each other. I don't think anyone has been sleeping very well. All these guys were chosen for a reason, and I have no doubt the council is watching us.

"Tomorrow's your official first day of training. You'll be woken up at dawn." Everyone, including myself, quickly undresses and lays down in bed.

Eventually, the dark room grows silent, and I can't help but wonder if the other men are sleeping or if they are staring up at the ceiling like me, wondering if they made the wrong choice to come here.

True to their word, they wake us up before dawn. "Get the fuck up and get dressed." When we don't stir, he says louder, "We ain't got all day!"

A sleepy, disorganized commotion ripples through the room as we all jump up and scramble to get dressed in the crappy jumpsuits provided. The worn fabric hanging from my body does little for my confidence, but it's no worse than what I walked in here wearing. I know the first thing I want to buy when I get out of here is an expensive suit because I'm done with having people take one look at me and decide how worthless I am.

"I hate our clothes," Ash says from next to me, and I have to fight the urge to push him away. I remind myself for the hundredth time that I may need an ally. I'll tolerate him for now, at least until I don't have to anymore.

We get to an old arena, and if the faded blood is any indication, they use this place to pit supernaturals against each other for sport.

"This business is not for the faint of heart." Tom's dark black eyes assess all of us, and his lip curls into a frown. He's not impressed. "Eventually, we will assemble you all into groups. We'll determine that later, but for now, we have to build up your stamina. Any questions?" He doesn't give us a chance to think of a question before he says, "Alright, start running."

I take off sprinting, not waiting to see if anyone follows. Since turning into a shifter, running is easy for me. I've been on the run since I left the brothel, afraid of anyone who seemed like they were tailing me. I thought it was Mr. Hank after me for the longest time, but when Ash told me the hunters were on us, it all made sense who I'd been running from all this time.

Tyler gets right next to me and grins, his stupid dimples on full display. He's taunting me, and it only makes me angrier. He looks around and back at me, his eyes glinting with a deviousness I hadn't seen before.

Knowing it's just us in the lead, he pushes me off the track, and I fall face-first onto the dirt. I get up quickly, taking off at full speed to catch up. I expect my wolf to demand his blood, but he's oddly silent as I catch up to Tyler and move to pull ahead.

As I'm passing on the left, I thrust my right shoulder into his to knock him off balance, letting him know I have no plans to be his little bitch here. Instead of falling over, he pulls slightly ahead of me and sweeps my legs out from under my body in a second. My life flashes before my eyes, and before I can catch myself, my face hits the floor, causing blood to gush from my nose.

"He tripped," Tyler yells. My cheeks flush as I look behind us and see all their eyes are on me.

I'm going to fucking kill that guy.

"You alright, man?" He tries to sound friendly as he extends his hand, but I push it away.

"I don't need your help," I snap and get into a sitting position on the dirt.

"Tyler, you're so fast, man." One of the guys pats his back, clearly impressed.

"Yeah, man, you were flying. I bet you could have done a couple more laps if you didn't stop here for Aziel." I want to flinch at the mention of my full name. I have to tell them to stop calling me that.

"Well, I had to make sure this wolf was okay."

"Fucking liar," my wolf shouts

"You alright, man? Ash walks up and sits down next to me." He evaluates my quick-healing nose and doesn't offer up the nurse.

"I thought Aziel was fast but you're quick. If I were you I wouldn't have stopped for him," the Orc named Leo responds.

"Yeah well, I couldn't let a fellow shifter stay down." They're easily gravitating toward him now.

The next thing I know, I'm on top of Tyler. I bring my fist to his face, but he's quick to block it. It's like he's had training. He knows how to fight, how to defend himself, and how to talk to people to get them on his side. This guy is perfect, which only makes me angrier.

Why the fuck is he here?

It takes three guys to pull me back. I shrug the other men off. "Watch your back," I tell him darkly as I turn around to leave.

I may not have grown up with my own kind and trained like these fucking people have, but I know what I'm capable of, and I will thoroughly enjoy ripping Tyler to pieces before I'm done here.

Chapter 12

Benji (1826)

It's down to one hundred and twenty of us. The others have been killed off. It's a ruthless place. Only one hundred of us will make it out of here alive, and I'm going to be one of them.

We've been training for almost four years now.

I've built more muscle and eaten better than I ever have before. I was sick the first few days from trying to devour everything in sight. I can't remember the last time I've ever eaten this good. Eventually, I slowed down trying to consume everything and so did some of the others.

If there is one thing I know how to do, it's how to survive. All these guys think I'm a pushover, and I hear them whispering about me behind my back. They wonder why I'm here.

What they don't know is that I distract them by singing. They think I'm only focused on having a good time and making friends, but in reality, I'm evaluating them.

I wanted to see who would make a good ally and who would most likely betray me. I have narrowed it down to three guys I can partner up with: Az, Ash, and Tyler.

Az seems unstable. He has a quick temper just like the other two. I think I'm much more mellow. Az is lethal. He's got a knife hidden in his shoe. I'm not sure if anyone has noticed over the years since he hasn't used it, but I've seen the way he reaches for it when everything is still and quiet. He doesn't trust the calm.

Tyler he's—he's really good, and when I say *good* I mean, he excels at everything. There is not one thing he doesn't know how to do.

Ash is holding back. I don't think anyone notices, but he's calculating. I usually try to avoid eye contact with him so he doesn't see right through me. I don't want any of them to know how serious I am about training or that I use my singing and humor to keep others from taking a closer look.

Ash has been glued to Az since they arrived. Each of them on their own would be considered an unstoppable force of nature, but together they are deadly.

That's why I try to be friends with Tyler. I know if we stick together, we can come out of this shit alive. I sucked up to him the day after our argument, we shook hands and that was the end of it. I don't trust him of course, but I've made an ally.

These other guys won't make it. They all might act tough, but they aren't. They've never had it rough—not like the four of us. I don't know the other guys' stories, but we are the only ones who never seem to fully let our guard down.

Az doesn't let anyone approach him, Ash is jumpier than any normal person should be, and Tyler always has something to prove.

The trainers have been working with us for years, but lately, our sessions have been harder than usual, and I know we're heading to our first assignment soon.

The men here are buzzing in anticipation. "So, what do you think our first assignment will be?" Tyler asks, sweat dripping down his face. We just finished sparring. He put extra energy into today to prepare for our first mission.

There's no doubt Tyler is the best at fighting. He brawls like his life depends on it every time, but maybe we all do.

"I don't know, but I hope it's killing hunters," I tell him, remembering the massacre at the circus. I may have killed the men responsible for using my sister and initiating the attack on my family, but there were so many more involved, and I can't wait to kill all of them.

It's lunchtime by the time we leave our room. Tyler and I are making our way to the dining hall when I see a figure lunging straight toward us. I prepare for the impact, but the blur of blond hair dives straight past me and tackles Tyler to the ground.

Az pins Tyler to the floor and pulls the knife from his shoe. He drives it toward Tyler's face with a look of determination, and I don't doubt he intends to kill him.

Tyler's hands shake as he grabs Az's wrist and tries to push the tip of the knife away from his face. His arms are weak from training, and I try to help pry Az off him, but he's stronger than I anticipated. Maybe he hasn't been giving his all during training like I thought. "Get off of me, Az," Tyler growls.

Az doesn't speak, only leans his weight into the knife and growls.

I look up to see if anyone else is here, and I see Ash in the corner smoking a cigar, watching us with one foot propped against the wall. On the first day, I never saw him smoke, but now it's a common occurrence that seems to have gotten worse over the years.

"Are you going to help or just stand there?" I ask as I try to get ahold of Az.

He pushes himself off the wall throwing his smoke to the side. "Let him go." Ash goes for his arm and tugs the knife away from Benji's face. Tyler takes the opportunity to head-butt him. Blood gushes from Az's nose but he's determined to finish him off.

I know Tyler must be exhausted from all the training. If he hadn't just been sparring, he probably could have taken him down, but I don't think that's a coincidence. Az is too smart and calculated to luck into the perfect moment. He's been watching Tyler train for years. I'm sure he knew it was now or never.

No one from the council is going to help us. They've been letting us kill each other off to get rid of the weak.

Az's hands are wet with blood from his nose, and the knife slips out of his grip. Tyler grabs it and stabs Az in the shoulder. He grunts loudly and falls back, allowing Tyler the room to jump to his feet.

"What the fuck was that?" Tyler pants, his eyes turning amber as his wolf threatens to take over.

"It's been a long time coming, you lying piece of shit! You think I would forget about your bullshit so easily?"

It takes me a second, but I think Az is referring to our first day here when Tyler took him down during the run. He made it seem like Az fell, and later Tyler confessed he'd felt threatened by how fast Az was. I never told Tyler's secret because I knew it would make him look weak and petty. He's my ally here, and it felt like his success was directly related to my own survival.

"Shit, man, that was four freaking years ago. You're still carrying that around with you?" Tyler stands up and extends his hand to Az. "You gotta learn to let it go." The panic he'd shown a moment ago is gone, replaced with a cocky smirk that doesn't help the situation.

"I'll let it go over your dead body." Az pulls the bloody knife from his shoulder and wipes the blade on the bottom of his jumpsuit.

These two are never going to be able to stand each other.

Chapter 13

Ash (1826)

I was twenty-two when the council's doors closed behind me, and I was a ball of nerves, scared of my own shadow. It was an unfortunate side effect of growing up with my dad beating me senseless just for existing.

The first guy I killed here, I had to picture my father's ruddy face when I took him out. I don't even remember the man's name or the color of his eyes. It's easier to tell myself he deserved his death rather than admit I killed him in cold blood.

He'd been sitting in the bunk beneath mine, rolling cigarettes and tapping his boot against the wall. I don't remember what he said when I'd asked him to be still, but I remember his blood soaking the bed sheets and puddling on the floor under my bare feet.

It was like I was sixteen and feeling my father's whip crack across my skin with every tap of his fucking shoe.

I killed him, and no one tried to stop me. The others watched me flip his body onto the floor and take the tin he carried his tobacco in for myself like some stupid trophy. I wasn't even a smoker. I just liked having something to do with my hands to pass the time here.

That night, I rolled a least a hundred of them with the man's blood splattering the paper in abstract patterns. Now it's a habit I can't shake.

When my nerves run rampant, I light another cigarette to keep calm. Every inhale now tinged with the metallic taste of blood that coated the first one I ever smoked.

It's barely midday, and I've already gone through a dozen while waiting in front of our beds for our first assignment. When Tom enters the room, what little chatter happening around me dies immediately.

"Keep it together," my wolf commands. *"We can't let them see any weaknesses, or they will eat us alive."* I know he's right. Only the strongest and bravest survive.

We've been hiding under the radar and only doing the bare minimum to get by. The same way I hid out of sight when my father was alive. I made sure no one knew how easy these training sessions were for me. I won and lost evenly, and no one suspects how strong I am.

Tyler and Benji seem to be the most popular out of all the guys. The background chatter is all about wanting to be paired up with them. I personally hope I'm not. I hate both of them.

I only tried to save Tyler from Az yesterday because my wolf was screaming for me to do so, not because Benji asked me to. But I've been sticking with Az. He doesn't talk much, and I like it that way. I've learned to sit in comfortable silence with him.

"We should pair up with the strongest of the group." Somehow my wolf already knows who it is, and I guess I do too, but I hope I'm wrong.

Everyone moves into a single file line, all of us standing straight in front of our beds.

"Today will be your first assignment." Tom walks the row of bunks and lets his judgmental stare drag over each of us. Theodore stands next to him silently. I don't think I've ever heard him speak before. He only shows up on special occasions, like when we have challenges. But he watches Benji, Tyler, Az, and me a little too closely.

Tom stops in front of Tyler casually as he speaks. "And whoever comes out of this alive will get to work for us. You'll be paid generously, and when your term is up, you can relocate wherever you want."

I normally don't care for Tom and his flair for the dramatics during training, but his words are the sweetest I've heard in a long time.

"Your first assignment will be retrieving a girl in Central America." *A girl?* "Capture her and bring her in. She works with hunters and is the one killing supernaturals."

"What's so special about this girl?" someone asks from further down the line.

"She's supernatural." Tom's reply is automatic like he rehearsed a response to all the possible questions we may have. "You will cover her eyes and mouth the first chance you get."

"What for?" I ask. It's such a peculiar request.

"She might persuade you to let her go." He looks over his shoulder at me. "She's going to play the damsel in distress. We've seen her do this before."

Benji licks his lips in anticipation. He's ready to kill anyone affiliated with the hunters. There is a rumor going around that hunters killed his whole family. If that's true, I can see why he's eager.

"Az and Tyler, you'll be paired up with each other." They both growl, but Tom ignores them as he hands us all folders.

I'm positive they saw the interaction between them yesterday. There is no way they think Az and Tyler will work well together. This must be another ploy for them to narrow down the numbers again.

"The rest of you find a partner. The first to complete this will receive an automatic job. The rest we will assess and see how well you've done."

I open the folder, glancing down at the two pieces of paper inside. One has a rough sketch of the girl, the second has information on her height, weight, and where she was last seen. No more is given.

"Hey, partner." Someone taps my shoulder, bringing me back to the present. I look behind me to see Benji's playful smirk. "I figured we can partner up together since *our* partners were paired up together." Fuck.

I turn back to look at the others, but I know Benji is probably the only one I can tolerate. "Fine. But no unnecessary talking." I've seen how much this guy can talk. I don't know how Tyler puts up with his chatter.

In the next couple of days, we get our clothing together and start our departure. When we arrive in Central America, we're exhausted. It doesn't help that it's hot and rainy in July.

We go around her last known location and show the locals her picture. So far, we haven't gotten any responses. They've all been dead ends.

Sometimes we will pass other groups in town, and I recognize the glint of hope in their exhausted eyes as we try to track the girl.

There's only one place here open for travelers, and all the other groups are staying there. Tyler, Az, Benji, and I decided to camp in the rainforest. We figured our best bet to find the girl would be to hold a position outside her last known location. The others are stirring up a lot of dust in town, and if she makes a break for it, we'll get her.

After swatting mosquitoes the first half of the night, I decided to change into my wolf and sleep this way. It's probably better to discourage other predators anyway.

The rainforest is no joke. What animals and shifters do to survive here is extreme.

I don't think Tyler or Az slept at all while they were trying to keep a watchful eye on the other. When the sun began to rise, they both seemed angry and unwell.

"Let's go hunt for food," my wolf says as our stomach growls.

I don't want to go out hunting in the jungle, but it's probably the best idea since we're about two hours away from civilization.

I watch as the others trail behind me in their wolf form. We walk together silently and in synchronization, just like a true pack.

We take pause as Az signals with his paw, watching him for orders. He's found something, so I let him take the lead.

A rabbit springs from the bushes, and I nearly pounce on it, but then I remember there are four of us to feed and only one rabbit. So we wait, none of us willing to eat without the others.

After hours of hunting enough for us all, we head back to our campsite, but what we find is enough to turn our stomachs upside down.

Chapter 14

Tyler (1826)

Everything is gone.

All my life I've been trained to survive, and as I stare at the space that once held our tent and clothing, it's obvious someone else knows we are here. We have to find the girl and leave with her today.

We shift into humans once we've circled the perimeter for safety.

"We need to find another supe who knows the area," I say, not even bothering to hide my nakedness as I search the remainder of our things littered across the ground for something to wear.

"There was a slight scent of jaguars. We should go back and check to see if we can follow the trail. Maybe they'll know something more than the humans."

"I saw footprints earlier, too," Ash says, automatically moving his hand to his side and going for a cigarette, only he grips them into a fist when it dawns on him that he isn't wearing pants.

"We'll follow Az, and if we can't find anything, we'll

track the footprints Ash found," Benji says just before he turns back into a wolf.

We all shift into wolf form again and follow Az back to where he first smelled the jaguar scent. We follow their tracks for hours until we come to a narrow clearing in the woods where a stream swallows their muddy paw prints. We're close to their camp; I can feel it.

Az shifts into his human form first, and we all follow his lead. No one ever claimed to be in charge of our group, but it feels natural and easy to follow Az, despite how much we've butted heads over the years in training.

Benji signals to us, and when we look in the direction he's pointing, I almost gasp loudly. It's the girl from the photo. I was hoping we'd track the jaguars and get some answers. I wasn't expecting the woman to live deep in the jungle with shifters.

Az motions toward a horse-drawn cart with bars like a cage.

Perfect.

I'm not even surprised the others from the academy haven't found this place. We all expected the girl to be with humans in town somewhere, not out here in the middle of nowhere.

I signal for Ash to follow me to the girl, and Az and Benji ready themselves to make a break for the cart. No one seems to need instructions.

Taking on our wolf forms again, I look around to count the shifters, knowing they're going to smell us the moment we get closer.

We only get one chance at this, so we have to get it perfect. If we spook the horses and they take off, or if the girl gets away, it's over. We're not likely to find her again. Capturing our target is the only way we have to secure our jobs with the council, and we've worked way too long and hard to walk away with nothing to show for our efforts. No matter how much I miss my mother, I can't go back to The Nightshade Growlers after all this time and ask for some shitty position as a laborer.

We watch her for a long time as she moves casually from one tent and out to another, smiling and talking with the shifters as if they are her family. She isn't one of them, but they seem so at ease with her presence.

A crying child with violet eyes breaks through the opening of a tent and clings to her, and the woman smiles fondly as she picks the little one up and settles their cries. The jaguars seem to keep an eye on her and the child, but not in the way you would watch a prisoner. They watch over them protectively, as if they were precious.

The woman sets the small girl back on her feet and pushes her gently toward a young boy approaching them, encouraging her to go off and play.

Our opportunity finally comes in the late evening. My legs are stiff from crouching, but I don't pay them any attention.

Our target heads to her tent, so we follow swiftly. I watch the cage move from the corner of my eye, knowing it's the guys bringing the wagon our way.

"Hey!" someone yells out, but Benji snaps his neck with one giant paw before he says another word.

We go inside the tent and shift back into humans. Sensing someone, the woman gasps, and I wrap my hands around her mouth before she can scream. She tries to fight me, but I'm stronger and keep a tight grip on her.

I bring her outside as she thrashes against me, and Az immediately rips the bottom of her shirt into long strips to bind her hands and cover her eyes and mouth.

Two shifters emerge from one of the tents, and I've barely seen the gleam in their green eyes before their bodies morph into massive black jaguars. When they growl, their canines protrude from their mouths, and they pace around looking angry.

Az and Ash shift to hold them off while I grab our prisoner and try to carry her to the cage, but she kicks my knee unexpectedly, and I go down hard with her struggling body on top of me.

Benji lifts her off me and tosses her into the cage with a loud thump, and I lock the door immediately as she lets out a pained groan around her gag. "We don't have keys to open it."

"Here they are," I say as I climb into the coachman's seat.

Benji tries to join me, but a jaguar lunges at him and sinks its teeth into his arm. He tries to stifle his scream while throwing the big cat off him.

With the reins in hand, I yell for the horses to step up, and the animals immediately start moving.

Another jaguar makes a long leap toward me, but I push it away just as its teeth clamp down on my forearm. My adrenaline spikes as my claws rip from my hands, and I rake them across the jaguar's snarling face to free my arm.

Az grabs the animal by the neck and throws him.

Benji sits next to me, claws out and ready to shred the next shifter who makes a move for us. Az and Ash teeter on top the cage, watching the jaguar camp fade into the distance. They keep their amber eyes focused on our surroundings, just to be sure there aren't any more followers.

There's nothing left of our camp to go back to, and its position was compromised the moment some strangers tore through it and took our things.

We're bloodied and exhausted, but we've captured her,

and the entire way back toward civilization, she thrashes at her bindings and squeals to be freed.

"We're going to scare the locals if we show up like this," Benji says, looking down at his naked body with a laugh.

"If you keep an eye open for other travelers, we might be able to find some clothes before we hit town." I tighten my grip on the reins as two figures move from the tree line ahead.

"Ask and you shall receive," Benji laughs, rubbing his palms together as he gets ready to pounce on the men with packs over their shoulders.

"Wait." I slam my hand into Benji's chest to get his attention. "Is that . . . What the fuck are they doing here?" Theodore and Tom are waving like old friends we happened upon by accident, still dressed in their Sunday best, not a fucking hair out of place.

Their eyes are full of glee as they see the contents of our stolen cage, and for some reason, their excitement makes my skin prickle.

"We found your clothes," Tom says, and he throws my belongings at me. I look at the others as confusion mirrors their faces.

"Did you take our clothes, Tom?" Az's voice is menacing like he's ready to rip him to shreds for taking our shit and making us believe our belongings were stolen, and frankly, I'm ready to strike him too. Most of my shit was replaceable, but the others didn't grow up the way I did. What few possessions they have mean the world to them.

Theodore eyes the prisoner like she's his next meal. He's too focused on the woman, and I don't like the way he licks his lips as his eyes linger over her ripped shirt.

"You did it. I didn't think it was possible. I thought her kind died out." This is the first time I've heard him speak, and his voice is hollow, devoid of emotion.

"I own you now," he continues.

"Wait, what the fuck are you talking about?" I jump from the coachmen's seat and land beside them. "This was a mission for the council. We didn't just do a fucking errand for you."

"I wouldn't do that if I were you." Theodore's grin turns evil when I take a step closer. His eyes are dark and unusual.

What the fuck is this guy? Something's not right.

"We've made a mistake," I tell the guys, taking a step back and trying to shield the girl. "We need to take her back." I can't tell what's really going on here, but it all feels so wrong.

My wolf is uneasily pacing back and forth. He senses something dark in our current situation as well.

"Yeah, I think so too." Benji looks like he's ready for a fight the way he angles his body. "I'm starting to believe she's the one who needs protecting."

Theodore has a strange black shadow following him. I don't know why I didn't notice this before.

"Make them forget all of this." He moves like lightning and is standing next to the girl's cage now. The next second, her cage is open and he's taking the cloth off her eyes. She stares out with hate, but what catches my attention are her violet eyes.

She shakes her head. "No."

"Why were we chosen to work for the council?" I ask. Something is not adding up.

Was this a coincidence? Were we targeted because we were outcasts, or is there something more sinister going on? I remember my parents always trying to be with me everywhere I went. Why have I never thought it strange that Silas showed up the first moment I had to myself in months? Did they know this was going to happen? Is this why the council insisted on us having no contact with the outside world while training?

No, this had to be their plan all along, and the four of us played right into it.

He grins. "There was a prophecy, but I wasn't sure how full of shit the sisters were when they said they had the gift of foresight. I was convinced they were wrong when I set eyes on you four, always bickering like children, weak little lap dogs who will never amount to anything. But her!" He wraps his hands around the cage's bars to get as close as possible to the woman. "A woman with purple eyes—mated to four. It's exactly like the sisters said."

"Huh?" Benji scratches his head, trying to figure out what Theodore is rambling about. We're all as confused as he is.

"What does this woman have to do with us?" Ash pipes up.

He turns his cruel smile at him now. "Did you know Krissy is a powerful witch? You had her in your hands all that time and never knew what she could do." All the color drains from Ash's face when Theodore mentions the name Krissy.

"How do you know Krissy? You leave her alone." Ash looks like he might be sick.

"It's too late for threats now, isn't it," Theodore laughs. "I will never let you four lead the shifter community."

"What is that supposed to mean?" Ash shouts, his claws ripping from his hands.

"Do it," my wolf interrupts. *"Do it now!"* he shouts.

"I don't know—"

"You have to. We're stronger together."

I sigh, this will either be a great idea or the worst idea my wolf has ever had.

We're already standing in a line together. "Hold hands." Ash and Benji look at me confused until they realize exactly where I'm going with this. Az doesn't look convinced. He watches me with wariness. He doesn't trust easily, especially after the shit I pulled when we met.

"Make them forget!" Theodore screams as he catches on to what I'm doing. He watches between the woman with violet eyes and the four of us. His hands are in fists, and the black shadows around him rage like the spiraling tendrils of an ivy plant caught in the wind.

"I accept to be part of this pack," I chant first, and the three of them follow and chant with me. It's a simple incantation wolf shifters learn as a child, and though I see Az looking between us with confusion, he mimics the words without question. "I take Az, Ash, and Benji to be my brothers and to protect them from harm."

We're all doing this fast in hopes we'll grow stronger together. I can already feel the spark inside me. My hands tremble with . . . *power*? Yeah, that has to be it. It almost feels like something inside me was dormant for a long time, and now it's sparking with life.

I turn my attention to Tom. "You led us to this fate and so you've led yourself to yours." I watch the blood pulsing in his veins. His eyes turn red as he screams until his head explodes.

"We're the Alpha's of the Iron Beast Pack," we say in unison. I can feel my brothers in every part of my being. It's so natural and right like the universe was waiting for us to acknowledge who we are.

"Interesting." Theodore rubs his chin in thought. He turns to the girl. "Make them forget what happened here. Tell them they've been accepted and report back to our headquarters in Washington state for their first official assignment."

"Not happening," the woman voices.

"If you don't, I'll find your family and kill them all. Thanks to these four, I know where they live now." He waves his hand at us, and I'm disgusted with myself. I should have seen the signs. I was so focused on being the best and securing the job, I let so much slip past me.

"I'm so sorry." She sighs, tears pooling in her purple eyes. "I have to protect what's left of my family." Before we get a chance to speak, she stands inside the cage and brings her hands up. "Forget you met Theodore. Forget you met me. You completed the challenge and came out on top. You are to report to Washington state for your first assignment. The only thing you'll remember is completing the ritual to become a pack."

I shake my head and look at the girl in desperation. Her violet eyes are the last thing I see before everything falls into darkness.

Chapter 15

Ash (1920)

I t's been more than one hundred years since I left here alone, and still, my stomach sinks as I walk the familiar cobblestone path with my brothers at my back.

Everyone we pass can sense our energy, and the crowds part for us, heads down, cowering in our wake as I head home at last.

I don't know what I expected to find in the place where my father's house once stood, maybe the charred remains of my abuser's body or a large black hole where his blood drained the soil of all life. Of all the possibilities I have imagined over the years, this was never one of them.

A fucking pub. It's almost funny.

I sigh as I stand at the edge of the property and stare at the rundown shit hole. They didn't put much love into building the place, but the Alphas always did enjoy shoving the most depraved members of our pack into the darkest corner of our society. I guess it's a fitting memorial for the life I buried here all those years ago.

A part of me thought I'd never make it back. We've spent so many years working for the council and doing their bidding. It was gruesome, but the money was a nice incentive, and we've accumulated enough to last our family forever.

We were the council's A team. When all others failed a mission, they called us in to finish the job. I didn't think they would ever let us go.

We've grown closer as a pack, too. No more trying to kill one another. I can't see them as enemies or rivals anymore, and I can't believe I ever did.

"Well, well, well." A familiar voice breaks over me, and my brothers stiffen at the sight of a woman leaning against a nearby tree. She doesn't look away or cower in our presence like the others, and when I look into her wide gray eyes, a new ache splits my chest in two.

Amara.

Pushing off the tree skeptically, she inches closer, trying to see if it's really me. Recognition lights the soft smile on her face as she glances up and down my body. "I never thought I'd see you again, but this?" She motions to my shiny new Oxfords and the expensive suit I wear with pride. "It really suits you, Ash."

She remembers me dressed in rags back when I was frail, underfed, and weak, but she's different too. She's not the same little girl trailing after Krissy and me anymore, that's for sure. Her long red hair lays in soft waves on her shoulders, and she looks more than taken care of. A pang of sadness hits me as I think of what her family must have endured in my absence, of what Krissy must have endured, but she doesn't look like she needs saving.

Before I know what to say, she's hugging me tightly, and as she pulls back, there are tears in her eyes. "Where have you been all these years?"

I grab her face fondly, looking at her like the little sister I never had. "That's a story for another time."

A look of protest crosses her face, but in the end, she says, "I'll hold you to it."

Amara pulls back and looks over my shoulder, still wiping at her face. "So this is your pack, huh?" Her smile once again widens as she looks behind me at my brothers.

Before I can answer, someone comes running from the stone path we'd just wandered down. "Ash, Ash," she yells out as she sprints toward me.

A man trails behind her looking out of place, almost recognizable, but once he lays eyes on me, he turns and disappears down the path again.

She jumps on me and crosses her legs around my waist before her lips are on mine. It's a strange and uncomfortable feeling. Since I've left here, I've fucked around with more women than I can remember, but this—this just doesn't feel right. I've never thought of Krissy this way in all our years of friendship.

"Krissy, get off of him." Amara rolls her eyes in disgust at her sister's display.

She looks at me and grins, and as she notices the guys behind me, her smile grows impossibly wider.

"Shit," my wolf says. *"I don't like the way she's looking at them."*

"Aren't you going to introduce us?" Krissy gets off me and goes up to Tyler. "Hi, I'm Krissy, and you are?"

My brother looks up at me before returning his gaze to the woman and smiling. "I'm Tyler."

Benji pushes Tyler and extends his hand. "I'm Benji." Krissy's eyes twinkle. Oh great, this is not good at all. We're sending the wrong message.

Az stands off to the side, trying to remain hidden, but it's hard because she has her eyes set on all four of us.

"Hey, what's your name?" He has his hands in his pockets, and I know he's clutching his knife tightly. I really hope she doesn't go in for a hug because Az will not hesitate to stab her if she takes him by surprise.

"His name is Az," I tell her, putting one hand on her shoulder so she doesn't get closer to him.

Krissy drags her eyes over to me. "Does he not talk?"

"Not to strangers." Benji laughs at my attempt at a joke. Apparently, I'm as stiff as Az when it comes to jokes. I guess I should leave the humor to Benji and Tyler.

My focus slides to the four newcomers practically stomping down the path. "So, you're here to try and claim my pack, you filthy trash," William spits. I didn't think he would still affect me, but my body flinches from the sound of his voice.

"Word travels fast, huh?" I manage to project my Alpha voice as the men push closer. "Brothers, this is William, Daniel, Jacob, and Ethan. Sons of the Alphas who disowned me."

Memories come flashing back in waves, and my hard exterior starts to deteriorate.

These four were my tormentors, my father's tormentors, but am I strong enough to go through with this?

What's going to happen when I try to kill them, am I going to hesitate?

CHAPTER 16

Az (1920)

Ash has been overwhelmed since we arrived, and I don't blame him. This place was both his home and his prison. The redhead witch looks at him with the teary eyes of a sister, but the clingy blonde they call Krissy has a different idea.

Her presumptuous kiss was a show to stake her claim over Ash as if the kind redhead were competition. Krissy watched us expectantly as if we were all supposed to fall in line for her affection.

That's not going to happen.

The others may have been distracted by her bubbly greetings and flirty demeanor, but I saw the man walking behind her. I couldn't tell if he was an Alpha here, but there was something familiar about the way he carried himself, and it was odd how quickly he disappeared.

Something feels wrong here.

I discreetly find the knife in my pocket as the others exchange bullshit pleasantries, sensing something darker that the others haven't noticed. Krissy is waiting for my attention, but I stare over her shoulder at the empty path leading into the woods.

My grip on the knife in my pocket only tightens as I see four figures emerging from the tree line.

"So, you're here to try and claim my pack, you filthy trash." Ash swallows hard before he responds, and there's a high-pitched ringing in my ears as a crowd begins to form around us.

"I want to rip their throats out," my wolf says, and I completely agree. I want to make all of them bleed, not just to take this pack as our own, but for the uncomfortable look on Ash's face that tells me these four are already under his skin.

The people around us appear starved and weak, and it reminds me of the way I looked when living in the brothel. The Alpha's here don't take care of their people, and when we slaughter these piss-poor leaders, I'll make damn sure this pack will never go hungry again.

They look at Ash with fear in their eyes. They knew he'd come back, though I'm sure they were hoping he died.

"So you think you can defeat us?" Ethan laughs, but his confidence sounds forced to rally his people behind him.

"Blood, blood, blood," my wolf chants in my head.

"If you decide to leave peacefully, we'll ensure your wife is taken care of." I nod at the lady with blonde hair and brown eyes who's standing just in their shadow, worrying her bottom lip.

Daniel looks at where I'm staring and moves to block her from my sight.

"Not a chance," Daniel says with a sneer.

I cackle out loud, and they all focus their attention on me.

"What's so funny?" Jacob looks at me with wary eyes, just like everyone else does except my brothers. Even when we were pitted against each other by the council all those years ago, my brothers have never looked at me like I was crazy. Ash stood by me the whole time, and now I've got Tyler and Benji by my side as well. I will never be alone, and knowing they accept me for my crazy, I would do anything for these guys, and I mean it.

Ash wants this pack specifically, so that's what we will fight for. We'll take this place and make it our home. The Alphas will submit to us by choice or by force, but if you ask me, I'd rather spill their blood than allow them to live here and plot against us.

I pull my knife from my pocket, and they all watch me with narrowed eyes. The people gathered around us are curious, but they keep their distance.

"Enough of this," I whisper and my knife flies through the air and lands right between Jacob's eyes. When he falls to the ground with a loud thump, everyone but Benji grows silent.

"Really, Az, you couldn't wait? Maybe they wanted to talk it out," he mocks because he knows just as I do, these Alpha's will not *talk*. They believe they have a chance at winning.

Tyler silently laughs as Ash stares at the floor like he can't quite believe what just happened.

Fuck, we're losing him. These men terrorized his childhood, and now what he's dreamed of is becoming a reality.

"No!" The woman howls in pain, but I don't feel sorry for her. It might make me brutal, but I don't care. My brothers will always come first. "Kill them!" she screams as she holds her dead husband. "Kill them all."

Ash doesn't waste any more time. He slams his fist into Daniel's face. He tries to grab Ash's neck, but my brother is stronger and better skilled at combat. It doesn't take long before his opponent is face down in a pool of blood.

The Betas are inching closer, but they know better than to

try and fight us. If they do, they'll be shamed by the pack. Although their body language says how much they wish to destroy us.

"We should toy with them." My wolf paces back and forth.

"I like that plan," I reply.

My grin turns wider until Ash ruins my fun. *"Don't."* That one word from Ash in my head has me immediately looking in his direction.

"Fine," I say back to him in the same mental connection we have. My wolf sulks in the corner, but it doesn't take long before he's back out and ready to fight.

The biggest Alpha tries to get under Ash's skin again. "Ash, all you are is a traitor. Son of a whore. Daddy's biggest mistake. You'll never be anything or amount to anything—" He doesn't get to finish before William's head explodes like a watermelon hitting the ground.

Chapter 17

Tyler (1920)

Everyone around us gasps. "What just happened?" A man voices. Everyone turns to Amara for some reason, but she shrugs. "Don't look at me. I didn't do that."

"Then who did it?" a female shifter asks.

"I did." Ash replies. His mouth twitches as if he wants to smirk.

Yes, Ash is back.

Three down, two more to go.

I'm ready to claim this place as mine. I can't wait to have a stable home. It's been a long time since I've had a place I can call home.

Krissy speaks up. "You four—" she clears her throat and raises her brows. "Have your own magic?" As soon as those words leave her mouth everyone gasps.

Az smiles like a maniac, and Benji winks at her playfully. I roll my eyes, but what catches me by surprise is Ash. He was basking in glory just a second ago, but he's realized this is real. He's wanted this for so long, and now that it's here, he looks unsure of himself.

"I don't want to frighten you," Ash speaks directly to the hundreds of people surrounding us. "My brothers and I vow to protect our people and land."

They don't look convinced; they look worried like we might cut off the blood circulation to their brains next.

"Don't listen to him. You all saw what he did to your Alpha, and they will do a lot worse to you," Ethan hisses.

The crowd backs up in fear. "We will protect you. You have my word." I try to talk in a soothing voice, hoping to convince them.

A man from the crowd steps forward bravely. "Why should we trust anything you say?"

"Your father was trash, and your mother was nothing but a whore." Ethan stares at Ash, and I try not to react to the words directed at my brother.

"You want me to kill him?" Az says through our link.

"No," Ash replies. *"I don't want to scare my people into submission."* I completely agree. That's not the way I want to rule either.

"The character of my parents doesn't define who I am. I was born an Alpha. I was born to rule. I was never given a chance here to show my talents, but if you let me, I'll show you a better life than what you've been living. No one will starve under my reign. I promise you." Ash's words ring through the silence, and I know the crowd is trying to decide if they trust him.

Some nod their heads in understanding, but it's mostly the rough-looking ones. The well-dressed and well-fed pack members look skeptical. "How does that benefit us?" a wealthy-looking shifter asks, and I assume he doesn't care if the lower members of his pack are starving so long as the famine doesn't reach his table.

"Dad," a young woman warns him, looking at Ash with

wide eyes. She's probably afraid her father's head will be the next to explode. "Not now, Brooke," he scolds, and I can tell she's contemplating whether to open her mouth or keep it shut.

"Ash," the man continues, unbothered by his daughter squeezing his arm. "We can all see you four are stronger than what's left of our current Alphas, but if there's nothing in this for us, we can always try to fight your rule. Is there anything you can do to sweeten the deal for those of us not worried about going hungry?" A muttered agreement rolls through the better-dressed part of the crowd.

"We've wiped out every pack in the northern territory. You guys can choose where you live. The territory would be yours. You can live among humans as long as you don't harm them." Their mouths hang open in shock.

"We've never been able to own a piece of pack land before."

"You'll be able to buy and sell your land just like the humans. We've got plenty of money, and we've already obtained the land." No one asks how, and even if they did, we probably wouldn't tell them where the cash came from.

The man watches each of us closely as he weighs his options. "The lands we buy will be ours?"

"All yours. Unless you decide to sell them," I respond.

He looks around for a moment before saying, "We're in." He kneels on one knee, and everyone soon follows suit, everyone except the Betas and the only two Alphas left.

"Traitors, all of you!" Ethan yells out.

Ash takes it upon himself to run toward the last Alpha, only his mouth growing and shifting into that of a wolf as he sinks his canines into the man's neck and rips it off with a loud crunch. Blood drips down his lips. He smiles, showing off his red teeth, reminding me that he's every bit as ruthless as Az.

"Only one more to go," Az says, staring at the wife. She shakes her head in horror and turns to run.

The Betas are now coming after us, but we don't waste time playing games. Those who stand against us will lie beneath our feet. Their pace slows as they realize their mistake and feel the pressure building behind their eyes. One by one, their heads go off like bombs, and the pure satisfaction on Benji's face makes me laugh.

"I love a chase," Az says through our connection.

"No," Ash replies. *"Let Laura go."*

Chapter 18

Az (1922)

The witch Krissy has been extra clingy lately. I've been trying to avoid her at every turn.

"Oh, Az." Fuck, she found me. Why can't she be like her sister Amara or any of the other witches?

I just want to finish my run in peace. She places herself in front of me, and unless I want to bump into her, I have to stop.

She pulls on my sweaty shirt, and when I only stare blankly at her, she drags her hands liberally up and down my abs.

I hate when anyone touches me. It brings back memories of when I used to work at the brothel. My entire body goes rigid as I fight the need to rip her throat out.

"We should kill her," my wolf demands.

"We've been told not to touch her, remember?" She and Ash used to be good friends when they were kids, and though their relationship looks anything but friendly lately, I'm trying to respect his wishes.

"I was wondering if you'd like to get a drink with me later." Oh, not this again. She winks at me seductively, as if I didn't know that *get a drink* was code for come over and fuck me later. I try not to roll my eyes.

I don't want anything to do with this woman, and I know the thought of a sexual relationship with her is enough to turn Ash's stomach sour. She just doesn't get it.

"Krissy," someone yells out, but she ignores them, leaving her lifeless gray eyes trained on me. I don't remember her eyes seeming so empty when we first met, but every day they fade a little more. I don't know how to explain it, but they feel hollow, dark, and cold.

"Maybe she's not used to hearing the words fuck off," my wolf suggests, and I can't help but chuckle.

"Look, this untouchable act is getting old. This is your last chance, Az. I'm not going to offer myself up again." Thank the goddess. I've been waiting to hear those words.

"Krissy," the male voice gets louder.

"Nah, I'm good," I say, wiping the sweat from my brow and trying not to laugh at her pinched face twisting with hatred. It's so weird to see such a beautiful face all bunched up like this.

"You'll regret this, Az," she murmurs, but because I have shifter hearing, every word sounds crystal-clear. She starts to walk away. "Don't forget to join us for tonight's festivities . . ." She turns around cheerfully like she didn't just threaten me.

"The pretty ones are always crazy," my wolf butts in, and all I can do is nod as she skips out of sight like the pretty little lunatic she is.

I finish my run and go straight home—the whole time my skin prickles like someone is watching me. I don't pay any mind to it because I already know it's Krissy.

The witches are holding a dinner tonight. Witches from all over the country are coming, and everyone in our pack is invited. It's a big event.

I've never been much of a talker, but I know I have to make appearances and talk to my people. It's part of being an Alpha of the pack. I actually don't mind it as much as I thought I would.

Since we became Alpha's, the witches and shifters get along well. From what Ash and Amara said, the Alpha's here have always treated her family and her coven like property instead of people. They were allowed to live here because it benefited the pack, but most of the other shifters were too afraid of the Alphas to befriend any witches. With the other Alphas gone, the stigma has been lifted, and the coven and the pack have unified.

There's lots of food, wine, beer, and desserts; I'm so impressed. Amara's bright red hair stands out from the crowd as she approaches and hands me a glass of Faerie champagne. She's worked really hard to make tonight happen, but instead of enjoying herself, she looks like she might throw up.

"So, what do you think?" She searches the crowd nervously.

"Amara." She looks back at me, a strange and fearful expression in her soft gray eyes. "It's perfect. All you have to do now is enjoy and relax." Her smile widens and her shoulders loosen up just a bit. I've never really had a friend outside of my brothers, but I'm warming up to the little witch.

"Thanks, Az," she says, looking at all her guests. "I'm going to make my rounds now. You haven't seen Krissy or her new boyfriend, have you?" I shake my head as she starts to look around again, the panic edging back into her voice as she mumbles something and disappears.

"Something doesn't feel right." I can hear Benji's thoughts before his footsteps approach.

"I know. I've been on edge all day. I went on a run this morning to calm down, but then Krissy showed up," I say, my free hand absentmindedly rubbing my stomach where I can still feel her greedy little fingers roaming.

He tries to hold in his chuckle. Knowing I hate being in her presence. *Asshole.*

"Yeah, I don't know what it is, but stay vigilant. I'm going to talk to the newcomers to see if I can pinpoint any bad intentions." I loosen my tight grip on the glass. I don't want to accidentally break it.

It's been three hours, and so far nothing out of the ordinary has happened. "Do you want another drink?" Tyler approaches with a refill in one hand.

One of the waiters grabs my empty flute while my brother hands me a new one. "Thanks," I say, still watching the crowd.

"Do you want to sit down?" he asks, standing next to me. He noticed that I haven't moved from this position since I got here.

"Nah, I feel more comfortable standing and watching over people. Besides, when I spoke to Amara earlier she seemed scared. I'm not sure what's going on, but something is off."

He takes a drink and sighs. "If you need a break from being the lookout, just let me know." I nod my head as he starts to leave.

Two more hours pass and the supes are drunk and dancing and just having a great time. My nerves are running rampant. My wolf paces back and forth. He smells the change in the air.

The music comes to a halt, and we watch as Krissy stands up next to the band. "Thank you everyone for coming. I hope you all had a great evening—" That's the last thing I hear before a high-pitched squeal threatens to shatter my eardrums. I squat on the floor and cover my ears, but when I pull my hands away, they're covered in blood. *What the fuck?*

I briefly look up and see everyone kneeling with their hands clasped over their ears.

My body starts to shake, and I can't control it. Something is going on, but I don't exactly know what.

When the ringing stops, there's no other sound, and the forest is too quiet. It takes me a minute to see straight before I can fully comprehend the severity of the situation.

Amara's high-pitched screams shatter the stillness of the night. "What have you done?"

CHAPTER 19

BENJI (1922)

"What have you done?" Amara's voice trembles with anger and fear.

In all the time I've known her, she's never sounded like this before. So broken, so empty.

What I see has me gasping in horror, almost falling back down on my knees, but I place one hand on the chair and one on the table to prop me up.

The scene before me is horrific. My body shakes as I'm hit with flashbacks from my last day with the circus. Just when I was starting to have a normal life.

This—this can't be happening again.

I worked for the council for many years, and nothing has triggered me the way this has.

The only word I can think of to describe the scene is a massacre. I promised myself this would never happen to the people I care for again.

I let them down. I failed them all.

The witches are on the floor lifeless, dead. While the shifters watch in horror.

There are plates and food all over the floor, and some of

the tables are lying in pieces. Maybe the shifters wanted to claw their way out of the noise; I know I did. The pretty decorations adorning the forest are now all over the trees like there was some sort of explosion, and maybe there was, but with the ringing in my ears, I couldn't hear anything else.

"Krissy?" Ash's voice is unsure, he doesn't sound like himself. He tentatively walks up to his long-time friend. "I don't believe you did this. Please tell me this is some kind of twisted joke." My brother's voice cracks. His eyes plead with hers to tell him this isn't real. Through our bond, I can feel his pain, and though I want to comfort him, another voice brings my attention somewhere else.

"Mom!" Amara yells out. I watch her run past me and fall to the ground, she screams and brings her palms to her eyes while she cries. Her raw emotions make me want to go to her, but I can't move, I'm too shocked to do anything but stare.

After a moment, she looks up. "Why'd you do it? Why did you kill our people?" She looks at her sister like she doesn't even know who she is anymore, and frankly, I think we all have the same look on our faces. I've always known Krissy to be attention-seeking, annoying even, but I would have never thought she'd be capable of such a vile act on her own people.

She smiles at her sister, but it's not the same grin I've learned to recognize. This smile is dark. "Don't act so surprised sister. I'm only taking the power that's rightfully mine."

I lunge toward Krissy in rage, but her voice cuts me like a thousand knives, and I fall to the floor again in pain.

It feels like something inside me is being ripped apart.

"What is going on?" I ask my brothers through our connection, but the words seem lost in the wind, and whatever they're trying to say is garbled and far away.

I try to gather my power, but I can't seem to reach it. It's slipping farther away. I feel like my fingertips are grazing the edges of my powers, but it falls right through my grasp.

"Wolf, wolf," I shout in panic.

"I'm here." A small amount of relief runs through me, but he sounds distant. I try to keep calm, but my mind is going into overdrive. We've done scary shit for the council, but this surpasses any scenario we've ever been in.

When the pain subsides and I'm able to get up, I immediately search for my brothers. I see Ash first, clawing his way up from the ground. I send a mental note to him, but there's nothing. Everything is blank.

I run toward Ash, but Az and Tyler get there at the same time I do. "Our powers and connections are gone," Ash says.

"Now, you four kneel," Against my wishes, my body does exactly what she tells me to do. I look at my brothers and they're sweating trying to resist the call but, in the end, we all cave in. "Perfect," she says before she disappears.

"Where's Krissy?" Az asks panting looking in every direction like he can sense her but not figure out where she's hiding.

"She's gone." Amara stands next to us. "She killed the witches to gain power, and she took away yours as well."

"Why would she do this?" I ask as I fall to the floor exhausted.

"I wish I knew," Amara sobs, falling to her knees in front of Ash and trying to gather him into her lap. "But I promise, I will help you find her."

CHAPTER 20

ASH (1922)

The morning is bleak and gray as the orange and red leaves blow from the trees and gather in piles atop the witches' graves. Hundreds of them.

Amara replaces the dried flowers on her mother's head-stone with a fresh handful of marigolds from her garden. It's been months since her entire coven died, and she still can't say her sister's name.

I come here with her often to lay new flowers because if it weren't for me coming back here, she would probably still have her family. My father used to tell me I ruined everything I touched, and sometimes I think he was right.

There's a woman off in the distance sitting by a headstone with her chin tucked tightly to her chest. I've seen her out here sometimes talking to herself, but there's a weird feeling in the pit of my stomach as I watch her today.

"Do you know her?" I ask Amara softly, and she cranes her neck to see the girl.

"Um, not really. I've seen her around, though. She was friends with a girl in my coven. But you know, the last

Alpha's tried to keep us separate from the pack. We weren't allowed to make friends with the wolves. If we did, flaunting it would have gotten us killed or exiled."

Amara stares at me as I watch the raven-haired beauty, and I can't shake the animalistic need I feel to get closer to her. My wolf is absolutely silent in my mind, searching for her scent in the wind.

"Would it be weird if I went to talk to her?"

"Couldn't be any weirder than standing over here gawking." She smiles and bumps my shoulder. "Go talk to her. I'll wait for you back in the car."

As the autumn wind shifts, her scent finds me and nearly knocks the air from my lungs. It's like pure electricity coursing through my veins as I move closer to her. When she notices me closing in, she stumbles to her feet.

"Wait, don't go," I say. Her top teeth sink into her plush lower lip as she hesitates, no doubt accustomed to the harsh treatment from the old Alphas. I don't know what to say, but I need her to stay.

I've heard about the all-consuming feeling that pulses through you the moment you first lay eyes on your mate. It just feels right, and as my wolf claws at every corner of my mind to be set free, I know he senses the same thing.

"Finally. We've found her!"

The smell of her fear mingles with the crisp air, and the spark of her amber eyes tells me she feels the pull toward me too.

"I knew you were out there somewhere. I just never realized how close to home you'd be." Emma steps into my body timidly. "What's your name?" I ask.

Her porcelain white cheeks flood with heat. "Emma," she murmurs. "I think you're my mate." She reaches out slowly and runs a finger down my arm, sending tingling sensations up my spine. My eyes flash amber as everything around me seems to intensify.

"Say that again," I whisper, hanging my head to brush my nose along her jaw.

"Say what again?" Her voice comes out breathy as I dig my nose into her neck, breathing her in and enjoying the way she squirms in my arms.

"The word mate. It sounds so fucking good on your lips." I feel drunk on the adrenaline coursing through me and imagine all the ways I want to claim this beautiful woman. "Kiss me," I say, gripping her chin and pulling her lips toward me.

On my darkest days, I was dreaming of this very moment, having someone to light the fire inside my empty chest and fan the flames until I finally felt whole.

I want to know everything about this woman, introduce her to Az and the others, and watch my brothers bask in her light. But I can't wait to taste her. I coax her mouth open with my lower lip, and she invites me in like I'm the sweetest thing she's ever touched.

A woman's laugh tears through the silence around us, and Emma pulls back in a hurry, instantly leaving me cold.

A wisp of blonde hair emerges from the woods, and Krissy stands before me with a wicked smile not reaching her cold eyes. "This is too good! I've been watching you all mope around here for months. It's about time something exciting happens!"

Emma cowers into my side at the sight of Krissy, and I instinctively step in front of her to draw Krissy's attention back to me. "After everything we've been through, why would you want to hurt your family?"

"Maybe I was tired of being the healer, fixing everything and helping your sorry ass. The moment you came back to me stronger and with your own freaking powers, you treated me like the shit on the bottom of your shoe. It's like the moment you didn't need me anymore, I was nothing to you."

"Krissy, you were never nothing to me, but I don't get to choose who I'm mated to. You know that. You were my best friend, and you were never nothing."

"That's right, wolves and their fated mates. I guess it's a good thing you passed me up then. The elusive mate really did exist for you all." She nods at Emma, but I don't like the way she creeps closer to us.

I glance over my shoulder for Amara, but I know she can't see us here from the car. Krissy cackles in response. "If you call for her, I'll kill her." I've lost my ability to communicate with my brothers, and I would never knowingly put Amara in danger as well.

It's up to me to defuse the situation, so I use my softest voice and try to reason with her. "What do you want, Krissy? I'll give you whatever you need, but no one else needs to get hurt or die for the pain I caused you."

"What do I want? Wow, Ash. I wanted you and the power we could have had together. It was always supposed to be us against the world."

"I'm not able to control iron anymore. You took those powers when you severed the connection between my brothers and me."

Her laugh makes me feel sick as she points to Emma peeking around my body, holding onto the back of my shirt.

"What a brave mate you've found. How will she rule over anything by your side if she's quivering behind your back?"

"Enough," I say harshly, and the smile falls from Krissy's face.

"Oh, Ash. I would have been a strong partner for you four, not like her. I still could be if you'd let me. You'd have your powers back, and with all the power from my coven, no one could ever challenge us."

Emma's hot tears are soaking into the back of my shirt, and my heart breaks at the thought of losing her so soon after I've found her. The guys would never accept Krissy, and after killing the coven, Amara could never love her sister again.

"Krissy, we can't—" Her shrill laugh cuts me off once again.

"You didn't think I was serious, did you? What use do I have for four little boys with no power? You couldn't even protect yourselves, let alone anyone else. I just thought it would be fun to hear you beg me to come back. I've been promised something much greater than anything you could ever offer me." Her eyes twinkle as I swallow hard.

The window to get out of this feels like it's closing. I shove Emma toward the road and lunge toward Krissy. "Run!" I scream, but a high-pitched squeal feels like it's going to fracture my skull, and both Emma and I fall to our knees with our hands over our ears.

Not again. This can't be happening again. My eyes squeeze shut without permission, and I have to fight my body to open them as Emma's terrified screams reach me.

"This is what I came here for," she says smugly, and I barely have time to open my mouth before she sends Emma's body into the air with a wave of her hands.

Emma kicks and screams my name over and over again, but I'm stuck on my knee, unable to move. "Stop, please stop. Ash! Please help me, Ash!"

"Krissy, please don't. I'm begging you. That's what you wanted, right? For me to beg? Please, don't do this to her." I haven't felt this helpless since I was a kid, and I hate it.

Goddess, please help my mate. I just found her, and the others haven't met her yet. Please give us more time with her.

"Krissy, look at me. I'm on my knees for you. Please, let her go. I'll do anything." I cross my hands together and raise them in a pleading position.

She doesn't care, though. The Krissy I know isn't there anymore, just a set of cold, empty eyes staring back at me.

With one loud crack, I watch as Emma's neck twists at an awkward angle, and the silence that follows her body hitting the ground sinks into every fiber of my being. "No!" I yell as I crawl toward her, cradling her lifeless body in my arms.

I'm screaming for her to wake up, rocking her soft body back trying to coax the air into her lungs. When I look back up in a panic, Krissy is gone, and Amara is racing in our direction.

When she lands on her knees in front of us panting, a choked sob tears from her throat. "She's gone, Ash."

I already know, but I can't let her go yet. I can't.

Weeks go by before I can look my brothers in the eye again. I had her in my grasp and let her slip between my fingers. They should hate me for what I did, for not being able to protect our mate before they even got to meet her.

Everything I touch falls to ruin. Death follows me, and to love me is to be plagued by pain and loss. I told my brothers they would be better off without me, but they keep saying this wasn't my fault.

I'm sitting with Amara by the fireplace in the home we took from the Alphas. She's poring over maps of nearby territories as she tries to channel enough energy to scry for her sister.

"What can we do to help you?" Benji asks from the door-way. When I look up, I notice his clothes are covered in dirt and dust from the construction in town.

He and the others thought tearing down the shitty pub built over my old home would help bring me solace after losing Emma. Benji's got big plans for a new club to stand in its place. Somewhere for him to play music again and something to create revenue and jobs for our pack members in need. They seem to think there's a lot of money to be made if we open it up to all supernatural beings since humans are trying to rid the country of alcohol. I'm sure prohibition won't last long.

"Seriously, man. Whatever you need to find Krissy, just say the word."

I smile weakly and light a cigarette, letting the smoke burn a path down my airway. This is the start of my pack letting me lead them.

They know I need control to survive the same way Az needs control in the bedroom. Tyler is looking for something other than fighting to keep him grounded, and ever since we lost our power to control the iron in blood, Benji's been learning to make bombs as a hobby. I guess he's determined to blow heads up regardless of magic powers.

"We're going to find her," Benji promises, sitting down opposite of me by the fire and watching me closely.

"I know you all will do anything to help, but when we finally locate her, she's mine. Avenging Emma is all that matters to me." I say, leaning my head back and blowing out a plume of smoke.

There is pity in Benji's eyes when he looks at me. He knows our mate is gone, and it hurts, but he and the others never felt the pull. They didn't feel her in their arms, taste her lips, hear her soft voice.

Her scared face and pained cries will haunt me in a way the others will never understand.

CHAPTER 21

TLER (1985)

"Happy Birthday!" My brother comes in way before I'm ready to wake up.

"Fuck off, Benji." He opens the curtains, the early morning sun peeking in through the large window.

"I got you something." He sounds way too excited, and I'm afraid to find out why.

He gets on the bed and starts jumping and chanting, "Get up, get up."

"Benji, are you a fucking kid?" I ask. Before he gets a chance to answer, I cover my head with my blanket.

"No way." He rips the blanket off me. "Get up and see what I got you." I sigh, knowing Benji won't stop. When he gets excited like this it's best just to go with it.

I know that lately I've been getting moody, and all my friends want to do is make me happy. I'm restless. I've trained my whole life to be in charge, and though everything is going great, we don't have anybody stepping out of line in our pack. The days we spend searching for Krissy seem fruitless as well, and it feels like I'm losing my mind trying to find my purpose every day.

I pull the sheets away from my body and come face to face with an uh— "It's a computer!" Benji shouts.

Ash and Az choose that moment to come in. "Benji what the hell! I thought we were all going to give him his present when he woke up." Az slaps Benji in the back of his head. Benji rubs his head with the palm of his hand while narrowing his eyes at him.

"You specifically told us not to show him until he woke up," Ash reminds him.

"He woke up." He points at me like it's obvious. I can't even be mad at him. I have to chuckle. I would've known not to trust Benji with a present, and I think they did too, but for some odd reason, Benji might have convinced them to tell him what they were giving me as a gift.

"Thanks, guys. I'm not sure what I'm going to do with a computer, but I guess we'll find out."

"It may help with your anger issues—" Az slaps Benji again. "I mean umm . . . it might keep you entertained." He finishes by winking at both of them.

They bring the rolling desk over to my bed and watch as I turn it on. They sit on my bed staring intently at the screen.

"So . . . what do you think?" Benji asks.

I look to my side. "I don't know. I haven't used it yet. I've only just turned it on."

"This looks boring. I'm out," Az says.

"Yeah, me too. Let me know if it does something interesting," Ash says as he leaves my room.

Benji stays close to me, staring at the monitor. I start playing Tetris and I'm so into the game I don't notice Benji pushing me off my own damn bed until I'm lying on the floor face-first.

I look back up at him. "What was that for?"

"I kept trying to tell you, but you were too focused on the game."

I roll my eyes, "What were you trying to tell me?" I ask getting off the floor as I watch him take the spot I was in.

He watches the computer as he answers, "Oh, umm . . . that it's my turn now." Fucking Benji.

(2012)

It's been years since my brothers got me my computer, and I've been hooked ever since. I build a space for all of my computers. Everyone knows not to come into my cave. Only my Beta, Matt, and anyone else I invite is allowed to come here. I've found computers to be relaxing, and that's exactly what I needed after years of trying to be the best at everything.

That's why I'm surprised when I see Az rushing in like he's on a mission. He walks right past me as he looks for a place to sit.

He finally finds an office chair and turns on the computer. I cross my arms watching him trying to figure out his next move.

Not able to take the silence anymore, I speak up, "Az,"

"Uh-huh," he says without looking up.

"What are you doing here?"

"I'm going to help you. I've hit a dead end so I might be more useful here."

Yeah, I don't know about that. "I've got this part covered, Az." Since getting my computer, I haven't been at the forefront of confrontation. I used to want to be the best at everything, but it's been a relief to let my brothers take control and let me focus on my hacking skills instead of fighting. Which, in case anyone was wondering, I'm the best of the best.

"I'm here to help." I sigh rubbing my temples with my fingertips knowing once he's gotten his eyes set on something, he won't give up until he's tried it.

I bring a chair over and sit down. "So what's our first step?" he asks with a furrowed brow.

Oh God, this is going to be fun. "This is not Apple software or Windows, we're using other systems," I explain to him the basics and there's a twitch in his eye already.

"So you think you got it?" I ask, knowing he zoned out after the first minute.

"Yeah," he says, grabbing the mouse while watching the computer intently.

I get up to grab my phone from my desk when there's a loud crash and I turn back around. "Az what the fuck!" I yell as my very expensive computer soars out the window.

"I'll get you a new one," Az says as he walks away in frustration.

Chapter 22

Benji (2022)

The tension in this house has been at an all-time high lately. Change is coming. Whether it is good or bad has yet to be revealed.

"Technology has made you weak," Ash taunts from inside our training ring.

Tyler takes a step back to assess his brother, a smile forming at the corners of his mouth.

"You think so, brother?" Tyler asks, clearly baiting him.

This is going to be a bad idea.

Tyler takes off his shirt, and although he prefers computers to brawling now, he's still carved with hard-earned muscle.

"I may not fight like you two," he says, pointing to Ash and Az. "But believe me, brothers, I still got it."

"Fight, fight, fight," Az chants the same way we used to at the academy. He's already bloodthirsty, and his pupils are dilating.

Well, I know he won't be any help.

Tyler ducks below the ropes and strolls into the ring to face Ash, his shirt tucked into the back pocket of his jeans.

Since he found his love for computers, he's been consumed with playing video games and probably watching porn to pass the time. I know I do.

Ash unbuttons his crimson dress shirt and lays it aside carefully with a smug smile. He's forgotten Tyler was the best when we were all in the academy. I enter the ring behind Tyler. There are no gloves. I look briefly at Az hanging off the outside of the ring, and his eyes sparkle with amusement. I'm more surprised when he says, "Don't do it, Ash. Tyler is still a beast, even if he does look like a nerd now."

I look at Az in confusion as he shrugs. "What? When Ash is crying like a baby later, I want to be able to say I told ya so." He knows it won't sway the guys from getting in the ring.

Ash doesn't pay him any attention, and Tyler only smirks. Both are shirtless, pacing in their corners and waiting for my signal. I put my arm up between them, and as soon as I bring it back down, they go at it.

I hop back over the ropes and meet Az outside of the ring. We watch with amusement as Ash throws punch after punch and doesn't land a single one. We are used to sparring against each other, but this is something different. Ash and Tyler both need to get something out of their systems.

They're both strong. There is no question about that. A long time passes before they slow down. My body feels exhausted, and I'm not the one in the ring.

With one lucky move, Tyler punches Ash right in the cheek. His face goes flying to the right, causing his whole body to fall.

"Well, I did warn Ash," Az says, getting up and heading to the ring. I follow right behind him. He crouches down and examines the bruise forming on Ash's jaw. "Ouch, that looks bad. You got him good, Tyler." I look in Tyler's direction as he leans against the ropes, clearly spent.

"It was a good fight to watch. I needed that." I laugh, moving closer to Ash so Az and I can pick him up and take him to his room.

I'm by his feet and my brother is by his head. As soon as we try to pick him up, he shakes us off. "I'm fine assholes," he shouts as he tries to get back up, but his body goes down again. I can't help but chuckle.

"I'm going to go shower," Tyler says when he's sure Ash will be fine. He limps his way out of the ring. I don't offer to help since I already know he's going to say no.

Ash, on the other hand, needs help to stand, and once Tyler is out of sight, he lets us pull him up. We carefully get him out of the ring.

"I almost had him," Ash growls, and Az and I try not to laugh.

"Sure ya did, buddy. It was a close one." Az pats him on the back as we drag him up to bed to rest.

CHAPTER 23

AMARA (2022)

"*Amara, wake up. Amara, my sweet girl, wake up.*" I turn over in my bed, hoping the whisper will quiet down.

I stayed out way too late at the Crescent Lounge trying to forget my problems at the bottom of a bottle, and now I need my sleep to recover.

"Go away," I mumble as I cover my face with my blanket. Whoever it is can come back later.

"*Amara, she's here.*" The urgency in her voice startles me awake.

This can only mean one thing.

My eyes fly open, and I immediately get up from my cozy bed, but I don't find anyone there, just a warm feeling surrounding my body. That's when I immediately know what's happening.

It's not every day someone in my family travels from the dead to the living and wakes me up. It's only happened three times since they passed so long ago.

"About damn time, Amara." I recognize the sound of my

aunt's harsh voice, no longer the warming tone she had when she wanted me to wake up.

How I wish it were my mother's voice. I yearn to hear her once more. I miss the hugs she'd give me when I was younger, and I feel so guilty about not protecting her when everything went down.

I've replayed the night my sister took our coven's powers in my mind so many times, it's like a bad movie I can't shut off. Krissy was in the strangest mood, chipper and excited one moment, and fuming the next about the silliest things the next.

We were setting up for the big dinner party, and the guy who used to hang around her showed up to help. I had always sensed something peculiar about him. While Krissy helped our mother hang decorations, he looked at me from across the garden with the darkest eyes, and the thick, black shadow around him caught my attention for the first time. His glare scorched my skin in an unspoken threat, and his lips moved in a hushed conversation.

Every alarm in my head was going off.

I spent hours avoiding the man, watching my sister hang off him in the most uncomfortable way, but when I caught him alone at the edge of the woods talking to himself again, I heard a low reply. That's when I knew what the darkness was surrounding him . . .

A demon.

He saw the recognition in my eyes, but with only moments until our guests arrived, I didn't know what else to do but go to my mother. Only she smiled and tutted her disagreement, reassuring me I didn't need to be jealous of Krissy's new suitor, that one day I'd be just as pretty and just as sought after.

I was so mad and disgusted by my mother's reaction, I

tore off to the house to cast a summoning spell of my own. Everything always came back to how beautiful and wanted Krissy was, and even our mother couldn't see the darkness right in front of her.

The demon I summoned that night was in a blind rage to protect myself and my snappy, ungrateful sister from the demon surrounding her stupid boyfriend. By the time I returned to the event, our entire coven was there, mingling with the wolves and having the best time.

My breath catches as I remember the dancing, the laughter, the easy banter with the Alphas. I had convinced myself that my mother was right; maybe I was just jealous of Krissy's new relationship with the strange, handsome wolf. I'd summoned a freaking demon, for Christ's sake.

When Krissy sucked the powers from our coven that night, the protection spell I'd cast when summoning the demon kept my powers intact, kept me from keeling over like the rest of the witches.

Krissy didn't know why I didn't die, the surprise on her face made that clear, but all I could think about was my mother on the ground in her pretty party dress, dead because I never realized she was in danger.

For months I wished I had died with the rest of them. It's been so lonely without a coven or family, and even though the guys have always tried to cheer me up and include me in their lives, I wonder if they blame me for not being able to stop Krissy. They lost everything because of her, their connection, their powers, even their fated mate.

They've become my brothers over the years, but when I look at them, I still feel guilty I couldn't stop my sister.

"Save the girl." My aunt's whispers become louder, and I almost want to cover my ears. *"Her name is Kat, and she has two teens. Save her, protect her. She's the mate of the Iron*

Beast Pack, but don't let them find out. They need to figure it out on their own."

I almost want to tell my aunt that she's wrong. Their mate died long ago, right before Ash's eyes, but I know the last time I questioned my ancestor's whispers, it took almost one hundred years for them to reach out again. I decide to stay quiet instead.

"She needs to find her weapon. Only one is in existence, and it's in safekeeping. She has to be the one to do it. She's the only one that can stop it from happening. She's the Chosen One." I swallow my cry because I know what her words entail.

Her whispers become low and distant . . .

"Go now and save her. Her curse is their salvation. She's the chosen wolf."

Acknowledgments

Thank you to my team of Betas Brenda, Faith, Karlie, Michelle, Nattiee, and Oriane for re reading this book all over again. Your suggestions help so much! I love you ladies! Thank you for sticking with me.

Thank you so much Heather! I know you had to deal with the hurricane, dealing with the groceries stores and you need to take care of your kids and you still came through. Thank you so much!!

Ari thank you for helping me keep my group active and reminding me of things I always forget. It's been a rough year and I'm so grateful you're sticking by my side.

My family thank you, thank you, thank you, for letting me write my books.

And to my reader's thank you so much for sticking by my side. I keep going because I want you all to get lost in a world where you everyday problems don't exist. I hope that I create that for you.

ABOUT ANGELICA AQUILES

Angelica Aquiles lives in WA state with her two sons, her husband, and her dog. She goes out fishing, hiking, and now offroading with her family. When she has downtime she loves to get lost in a good book.

Join her FB Group:
https://www.facebook.com/groups/1107819209697422

instagram.com/angelicaaquilesauthor

goodreads.com/angelicaaquilesauthor

amazon.com/~/e/B091QFG3Y2

bookbub.com/authors/angelica-aquiles

9 781955 524094